AQUAMARINE

Peter Pessl

AQUAMARINE

final tales of the revolution

TRANSLATED FROM THE GERMAN BY MARK KANAK

TWISTED SPOON PRESS • PRAGUE • 2008

Copyright © 1998 by Peter Pessl and Ritter Verlag
Translation and Preface © 2008 by Mark Kanak
Copyright © 2008 by Twisted Spoon Press

All rights reserved under International and Pan-American Copyright Conventions. This book, or parts thereof, may not be used or reproduced in any form, except in the context of reviews, without written permission from the publisher.

ISBN 978-80-86264-28-8

This translation was made possible by a grant from

BUNDESKANZLERAMT ⁞ KUNST

CONTENTS

Translator's Preface	9
The Electric	13
Out of the Apple Garden	37
The Two-Headed Breadlady	59
The Bath of Little Lovers	81
"Of a Desert Day"	113
Have Mercy On Us!	131
Revolution of the Intimates (a Report)	141

TRANSLATOR'S PREFACE

Peter Pessl's *Aquamarine* in its present form is the result of two years' musings following the author's long and twisted journey (both in terms of pathways and encounters) to Mexico in 1993. After having been variously reworked, the volume was eventually published in German in 1998. Considered groundbreaking in form and style, the novel is composed of seven intertwining tales whose unsettling, exceptionally ambivalent female protagonists, "Aquamarine" and "Marine," crisscross diverse Mexican landscapes and cities of both external and internal geographies much like a madcap road movie plowing straight through historical episodes into present-day reality. Along the way we encounter the horrific tragedies of both private and political worlds as the tales channel into a common stream of storytelling that is so immediate in its presentation it violently impacts the very language itself (and the imminent possibilities or impossibilities in Pessl's use of language). The reader is thus swept into a swirling dreamscape of words and images, a ramshackle narrative construct where every kind of reality that is, always was, and will continue to be exist simultaneously.

In his attempt to rediscover and redefine a new kind of storytelling itself, Pessl revisits Mexico's many periods of catastrophe: colonial rule, violence, abuse, poverty, genocide, and political terror. All are revealed in a sort of dark, flaming thicket of imagery that is the heart of the text, a disconcerting puzzle, pieces of a whole spread out in confusion and madness with the final, brief tales breathing into life via a kind of *floralen Sprechen* (flower speech): entirely self-contained, the disjointed characters oblivious to external influence or the noise of the world around them. This abstraction (a sort of broken mirror reflecting the hot Mexican noonday sun), culminates in a hybrid "metalanguage" that expresses various high points followed by tentative conclusions as experienced throughout the the journey itself.

Pessl has truly developed a linguistic style in German that is unique to him, and it is his approach to language, his innovative experimentation and precision, that caught my attention when I first read him some years ago. Of course, these days the word "experimental" is too often bandied about, and it usually leaves us disappointed that what appeared as dynamic form is little more than mere structure. In Pessl's case, however, the reader is caught up in the hypnotic flow, the play of dialogue that inevitably entices us (as all good books will) to keep reading. The windings of Pessl's language thrust the reader into a subterfuge of chatter, a transmission where we can imagine ourselves frantically twisting the tuner dial (to invoke an archaic age) to listen in on bits and pieces of a program, maybe a radio play, a tale, a history that taken at face value is too much to bear outright — an ambling dialogue of waking dreamscapes that are hypnotic, cumulative, and ultimately beautiful.

MARK KANAK
March 2008

Mexico, Steiermark, Latium
1993 / 94 / 95

THE ELECTRIC

"We can't see out these lemon-colored windows, but still, we see revolutions. We cannot see out of these lemon-colored windows (of a crying being) hovering before our eyes, following the crying, and yet we see everything. What a joker! Lenin coming toward the bridge. Modalities. Only then, the New. The Applied. The petite squandered. The dissection. That which went before and that which is to come. Deficits in legalities and smell of the river coursing through the smoking present," says MARINE.

"If we have a look at the past (black) revolutions and the future (red) revolutions, we are sitting close to the bulkhead, our legs covered with an amber-colored blanket, the body-revolutions that are bodily forgiveness and prose forgiveness and a wasteland of little human developments that unfold beneath the weeping cusp of the visible right up to a metamorphosis into the Electric," he says in the weeping Selvas, if one thinks, "we commit every crime. We traverse the line of crime, a step beyond the gentle, right into a shredding. When the axis of political incision touches the axis of the aesthetic in the twilight of the criminal. We are continuing along the path to a shredding of laughing puppets of a final revolution."

AQUAMARINE answers him:
"We're standing within an indescribable story; we go, we sit, we sleep, we see and we are seen, we hesitate, we are silent, but we are standing in the midst of an incomprehensible and impenetrable story that cannot be severed from experience, from the freedom, beatings and holdups in this deviant present and within an impenetrable existence (cargo), and as momentary Electra each within another incomprehensible body, powerless, frail and free, revolutionary-counter-revolutionary, resting on an arm, like a dog, amber, a daughter of minimal beauty.
This story has a brown brushed body of a white, feminine child. What an odd one. I am a bridge 'end'. Modalities. We're carrying yellow cakes in our hands. The petite New. The electric. Cakes, they've been formed from river water and river sand and we eat it in the morning and in the evening too, they have a slight human form and 'show' men and women. We cannot see out the lemon-colored doors of a weeping human being, and outside the incomprehensible storm of revolution blows on. Of the black. Of the red. Of animal-coal. Of mountains of corpses. The old. That which came before and that which is to come. A rebellion against the visible that does not concern us. The momentary — it is not visible, it is electric. It invests."

"We are happy (modern).
Milkmen. Train. Bearers of bread.
Furious in contradictions.
But nothing is more difficult.
We need the incomprehensible, not of milkmen and the impermeable (vacant) of the train and a balance of bread bearers (retro) in order to be happy. We have our own (petite) differences. We have everything else, without choice, in our heads. We have everything else, without choice, that's medicinal milk. Sitting, we're sitting in this indiscriminate river or under these transitory trees alongside illuminated or non-illuminated toucans (Lenin), digging in the slime for edema, powder and bones," says MARINE.

"If we wait a long time in this incomprehensible moment, bright body parts shall emerge (in elegant conditions), and whole cadavers, too, lightworks on which white herons are standing, and crows, lilies, animal modalities, moving right past us, feet crossing over bright river bottoms, now, and then, from one reed-thick shore to the other."

AQUAMARINE answers with a reply to the visible in the Selvas:

"The 'electric river' is the New Thing. The Momentary. Invisible.

The 'revolution' is the Old Thing. The Visible. The Applied. The Small, the Squandered. That which went before and that which followed. For which a life was lived.

If we're not attentive, these things will become visible, as well: 'The Child', the birds, 'the Birds' in this river story, in an impenetrable river tale of the Usumacinta, 'The Doors', 'Trees', 'Slime', 'Edema', 'Bones', 'the Floor'. And we'll mix them with river slime and river water and dissolve them. We'll throw the revolution into the river. And then, when we have dissolved the visible and its amber bodywork in an oval sand cloud in the Usumacinta, then the story will begin. The story we're talking about is electric to its very core. A daughter of minimal beauty. To be told in a river, standing. It lets the listener tremble. From the cold. From ferocity (present). From stillness. Beginning at the poles of the hand. In a final chemistry. It emerges from a mix of that which went before and that which follows in the electric water of a transient river. It is transient, and invisible. And yet — nothing is more difficult. Of all the roaring possibilities. Logic has been set in this water music. We are lost. Oh to be forever lost. If one had ever lived. In being so, that we had always been lost, and in so being, saying 'river', and seeing all rivers in a final defining moment. Equally, counter-rivers. Unto the offset, the trade-down, the effort. The final story, white, shuddering in mystification!"

"We go back and forth in the howling Selvas, no personal animal speaking there, but we see cows (that's how I say snow), but we don't see out those lemon-colored windows of that ship that's gone ahead. And we have this ship that's gone ahead, and it will also be that which follows, and for a moment, if we dissolve it in the river, the electric, enter the river Lacantun and have gone to the blurring Usumacinta on a faded, tired platform ship," says MARINE.

We, present, under this platform ship.
Thus I say snow.
Thus I say heaven.
Of enormous proportions.
Thus I say sunflower.
As obfuscated as what I saw; the platform ship. It was impenetrable. In sorrow. Bearers, traverses, sorrow. Then, that which followed: the knee. The rabbit. I dissolved all of them in the water, they sank in brilliant muddled clouds right down to the river bottom opposite and were electrified. I could no longer touch them. Medusa. I grabbed the rabbit by the 'spoons' and shuddered in this story that strives to and completely achieves an end, and I grabbed 'the white story by the spoons' and dissolved it. A hydra. Resting on an arm, just like an amber-colored dog does. A piranha. I sawed the story into pieces and dissolved it and its beginning. You tiredness. I dissolved it in an electric river. My time has passed. Just as small, impenetrable time passes us by.
I'm standing up to my belly in the sluggishly flowing Usumacinta, I'm carrying a mat made of bast on my back that has the shape of a piranha or a tapir — and always that

of a star. And of a rhombus. My time has passed. In my white hands I'm carrying a human shaped cake. AQUA-MARINE tells me it looks like: the chancellor. The capo. The president. I've bitten off the heads and am chewing them gently. You tiredness. AQUAMARINE sticks ants and wasps down to their waists into the animal mat on my back with a glass tube. She's carrying rue. She's blowing a white pipe of bone. Nut clatterers beat on my knees, their noise scares away fish and crabs. Just imagine what's possible if you think. My time, which has past, was always without any context.
Toucan feathers whirring against my shuddering body. Deer hooves.
Lenin.
Certainly not Lenin.
You know what I hear? 'You tiredness'.
I'm submerging these brown figures with slightly human form beneath the blurring surface of the river. I understand. They dissolve there and sink to the bottom in twisting cloudiness.
I, the owner of something moveable.
That which went ahead and that which followed — dissolve.
It's simple. I could show it. It sang.
Those present assume a river shape, a mild river odor, it's electrified, they radiate, they swim beneath the surface of the numbed river and can no longer be touched. Not that one.

I've awoken these small people within a white story in as much as I've touched them. They were electric. A fine dog. I, shuddering within the story.
Thus I say 'snow'.
We are lost within these enormous proportions.
Thus I say 'heaven'.
'Chancellor', 'capo', 'president'.
The dissolution of these slight human shapes formed from the slime and water of the Rio Usumacinta have initiated their appointment unto heaven. The misshapen chancellor. The cutting capo. The snowed-in president, that invests.
I brought her, this river, to that point where they go, in tiredness, in sleep, remaining quiet, weeping, hesitating and traveling back to earth as lightning and as a blizzard of human revolution. This human revolution of which I'm speaking speaks of those human forms that've been freed in heaven. Only that. But this, too, is further misused as a rebellion against the visible. The small. The blocked. The momentary-human corresponds to the stars. To the rhombuses in heaven. A new revolution shall report of those who've been released. Reducing the obstructed and transporting the dead to "heaven" in that through killing, devouring and dissolving on this blurring river; there, they are illuminated, as reflecting stars. Where my Sunflower wishes to go.

I cannot say that the Electric has followed me through weeping woods. It hadn't occurred to me to think of weeping, much less storytelling. I cannot say that the woods have become electrified forests along the lines of a crime, as it were, nor that I have dissolved them in the amber-colored river; I cannot say that the Electric has left a river wallowing in my hands, enclosed before my chest, with the rhombuses; I cannot say that the Electric has left a certain river and river displacements and followed me, such as: dog, rabbit, or hand. In dissection. Of a dog that went ahead through a hand following in parallel. In a momentary-rabbit that flees into the wood. Of an exact severity of calling. Of a final severity and gentleness in the example of incision.

I've grasped at the trees: they were electric. I was running away from love. I touched maritime cornfields in passing, and they were called 'severity', 'counter-severity', 'sole direction', 'exorbitant', 'temperate', and were anemic. Oceans were investments. Barrels. Oceans were the next possibilities in the far-off distance. And then the rhombuses. The seven-pointed, in dissection. Chinese kites. Flying through the air. And flying chill. 'Sole direction'. 'And chill'.

We were drawn across the sky.

We were drawn through a chill was in itself utter contradiction.

It was victorious. In me, it was a barrel, before me and

behind me — and within me as well.

'The barrel' I said, and it disappeared after precise invocation and became smaller. I treated 'the chill' in the very same way. It became smaller. The Electric passing through those enormous proportions. Like chill, in flight. It's a contradiction. It seeped through my brown shoes, and I said, 'brown shoes' and they were within me, gone against the mountains, opposite, and I said: 'Opposite smaller mountains', often surprising, and they were lost within me, and I took all the mountains of the Selvas landscape with me, into that pattern and into final dissection — and it's just not possible to find them again, no, for that would have to be accomplished with the assistance of amber-colored, all encompassing chill. In summer it came as lightning, calling: 'we're bearing down just before these hills, just opposite', or 'banknote lightning', 'love-gentlemen-lightning', and went before the people as a burning, whining city, and in winter the Electric came as snow and left as a break in the snow, into the forests. For me, there remains *flint*. And the models. We are lost within these enormous proportions. Scale.

We are exchanged, one for the other, smaller, 'garden' for 'head', 'head' for 'finger', 'finger' for 'nail', 'nail' for 'a single piece of yellow corn'. Thus we become smaller and disappear into atoms. Into the sub-atomic. And in the end, into the non-visible.

We exchange blows there. Decisive blows. 'Precisions'.

Distributions. Accounts. Ergo. Without conscience. Without the mildness of the beginning. Yet with the mildness of snowfalls. Points, victory in little; an impenetrable time that passes. Weeping. Just as we initiate relationships (to words) and as we break them off. Colorful blows to an electrified head. But meaningful. Yet meaningless. Tortured.

I situate myself between electrified trees, they're mangos, the light 'green' and 'red', cable about my head. Green cables. Serpents. Meandering lightning. Poles in my hands. Blows exchanged until we scream: 'The non-visible is growing! Contradicting! The electric is growing! It colors us green and red and we're getting smaller!'

I can say that the electric, police-women plasma has me. I can say the Electric is speaking. If I lift my arm, I ought to do it, hills facing opposite are hanging on it and the electric, it's aglow within my lamp. I carry it with me, everywhere. I carry it to the war-people and they obliterate it. I bring it into the inbetween-rooms of the political. It warms strange heads there. I call it: 'lamp', 'in which', 'lamp-in-which'. Still, it does not wish to remain. *Amber* serpents. It's nothing, and no one. Smaller. 'You tiredness'. It's the lime before my closed eyes. The blossoming hazel. There, where there ought to be only mangos. The Electric does not desire to remain constant, no, it flickers before it flees and shows a lime. Bright newspapers. It shows the completed equation: 'Bright newspapers of a

lime'. I can say that the Electric speaks in equations. Set up, in the non-visible. In atoms. With the war-people. With great engineers. After great nature that speaks in murderous equations, speaking of shootings and extractions of the spirit, of suppressions, of seasons' walleyes.
The fish of the blurring Usumacinta accompany me through the meandering forests. Crabs at my heel. Piranhas at my calves. But I am current (racing). Crabs determine neither the luminous present nor the political. Berlusconi. Fini. Crabs of voraciousness. I take fish and crabs with me, I strip them from my legs, I put them in my pockets in that true and real childhood of Formosa, it strips them away, back to the mango trees, to a true and real childhood that begins to sink away, in my brown pocket, I take them with me into great parables that encompass and cut through nature, I clean them there with brown shoes and serpents, throw them into firewater and enough! I strip them away into the great equations of an ocean that invests. They speak very quietly. But they speak according to nature. They die ideally and according to nature that contradicts.

"Real youth is painless. It turns away into the lime," says MARINE.

"Real childhood is painless. Soapy form. It moves, back toward the mangos. To the Chinese dragons. And the same sorts of lanterns," answers AQUAMARINE.
I'm some distance away. In an electric garden. 'The fur hat'

enters the story. And disappears again. Also, 'Murmansk'. And returns again to an electrified Baltic. After the Soviet collapse. Soon, it gets 'cold'. I can say the electric passes through the garden set on a height in the Mexican jungle above a loop of the Rio Usumacinta and warms it. Rhombuses. Snowbrooms. Passing time in small, lily rhombuses. You prove 'the senseless' to me. 'The meaningful'. 'You tiredness.' 'You!'

I stand in front of a garden with a amber-colored dog and say: 'I am standing in front of a precise garden.' That's enough. You tiredness. The light is weak. The precise light has become weak. The wolfhound. You. You garden-dog. 'I'. I!

I am even yet carrying white and green cables wound round my head, 'the exact electric' flowing within. The fabulous. The tragedy. Electra. A severing and collapse of every perception. Or near-perception, as we thought of it. The electric helps me throughout the story, these stories, 'the exact electric' helps me to speak the story just-so, just as it ought to be: with meaning. Senselessly. Truncated. Fleeing. Singular. Decagram. In equations, with lilies. Equations. Heads of government. Remembering the lime and the torn dragons within it. A yellow scarf. Yellow collapse.

Right up to the yellow collapse of a precise person, with a lamp, in a precise garden that blooms and freezes over. That expands and contracts before closed eyes. Precise drowning. And contradiction. Interference. Of words. Rhombuses. Seven star. Synchronism. Hard blows. Left. Right. Diagrams. Smoking eyes.

"I am not visible," says AQUAMARINE.
"These two ideas about me, one I would refer to as 'weeping reason' and the other I'd call 'the racing irrational', these two ideas of me, in the distance, lead me far beyond the visible."

"The wavering. The exact," answers MARINE.
"The wavering and the counter-wavering. So great and masterful, this reason. So great and masterful , this irrational thought."

You see, I'm relating how I am going. Moving. Wavering. Hesitant. One leg auditioning, the other remaining behind.

'Milk'. 'Ridiculousness.'

'Principles'. 'Spoons'.

I become acquainted with legs. And blurring words. Anti-words. River-words. And assistants. Rashes against freedom. Rashes for freedom. We throw revolution into river. We've fled three days and nights from revolution, into whining cities. Into the green matrix. Revolution. Counter-revolution. Always, both ideas. That's enough. We didn't wait until we would've been found in Boca Lacantun, no, we smiled at the forests standing opposite us. We blinked. We used the next-best crane ship up the rolling Usumacinta, we paid, and I said: 'Of our own precipice' and 'of duplicated milk' to the crane ship captain.

We have the obligation (milk). We have ridiculousness. We must escape obligation. So strong is this reason. So strong is this irrational-milk. That's enough. We said:

'That's not a skirt! That's not a revolutionary skirt you're wearing!

You're moving backward!

You're wearing a vermillion coat with a reed on the proscenium, and spitting!

The curtain.

You're going back.

You trip and fall back down into the story of monkey-theater. Handgun. Of the idiotic.'

Momentarily we've fled from the captain and sailors' shots and screams into the weeping Selvas, having had no good intentions, no, we do not want to get ahead, nor to go back. They would've killed us for that alone. We retain the rudiments. Honey.

Why? Honey-why. Honey in the Mexican revolution of '93. Dead like honey. Murder like honey. Pistoleros. And in the capital city, like a blossoming honeyman.

The revolution limits itself to heat and precise gardens. It's a word-revolution, if we think about it. It's nothing more than a blossoming word-revolution. But we dare not utter it. The revolutionaries, they worry themselves with 'the children', 'the mothers', 'chalk in the streets', 'safes'.

Liquors. We dare not utter it, they take it quite seriously. Much honey in the faces. Honey-why. Much milk in the hands. Milk-why. Slopped about, the whole thing! Drink down destruction! How late is it? Sitting dog? Just in front of the precise headquarters of the party? A dog-party? The ultra-party? We laughed that, that's enough. 'You'. 'I'. You! I!

The petite, that would be the task for a revolution if we should think. But they want it otherwise. They are freeing London, Budapest, and Paris. How late is it now? Mexico City? Dead dog? Tacuba? Puebla? We've talked about it for days, the captain, the sailors. We'd say: 'Smoking captain', 'blossoming sailors'. They'd answer: 'Weeping refugees'. Fleeing from a word-revolution. Into a green matrix. We tell the sailors about tragedy. Electra. When was it? The tragedy of reason. The dislocation. We're speaking about precise tasks of the destructive against the body, against the visible, against mourning. 'Sudden rain', 'the captain', 'the precise captain'. The precise captain says: "Milk, desperate milk-exactitude, that's proof for the distance of the body, and we'll keep it. The rest will be burned."

We're speaking about freedom and milk.

We're going to the precise. Into the most precise, into the Arab. Into the mosaic.

We are speaking about precise revolution, and milk.

The last mosaic. Net of precision. At a construction site.

In the Selvas, if we think about it.
If we think about it, though, we would be lost.
What's said to me about milk, about weeping rivers, about honey, about precision, if I think about it. That which is told to me is thoughtfully precise. 'The Arabian revolution'.
For example. Precise and pointless. Meaningful. But precise. I'm afraid. Come!
We've fled right through the blurring Selvas, we've crossed hills, rivers, we never saw the Usumacinta again, never found it again, the precise captain, the blossoming sailors. We were in agony. For words. What did I mean by 'hills', by 'rivers'? What are 'toucans'? Who is 'Lenin'? We've found the deepest center of the racing Selvas. After we'd quietly inquired. What we found was: Possibilities. Alternating possibilities. Facts. Alternating facts. Making up the innermost, bloody mechanisms. Blows come from there. Counter-blows. The storm. The bloody collapse. Pressure in the boilers. Steam in exploding heads.

AQUAMARINE says:
"There's the diagram. The precise. There's the great, killing diagram!
'Go!'
'Sleep!'
'Wait!'
'Laugh!'

MARINE answers:

'Sleep-milk'.

'Go-dogs'.

'Wait-milk'.

'Laugh-dogs'.

We must bend the senseless (milk) and the meaningful (milk) together in a diagram of weeping. Of counter-weeping. Of silence. Of tiredness. Of racing silence. But I'm tired. We'll take both bloody poles of the world in our hands and clap them together. And thus, a blizzard. Lightning-strike! And thus, electricity. We'll find the most internal of subtle detonation. If we simply say: 'Sleep', it's open. If we say: 'milk', it's open. We *have* to say: 'Sleep-milk'. If we slap both bloody poles of the earth together, and it succumbs in a final tiredness, in a final collapse, and it surrenders, it falls into an amazing sleep, and it causes a thorn, and loses any terror. What we've found in the roaring Selvas is: The condition. Without living the terror. In terror without example. In a slumbering blizzard. We've gotten used to it. We're speaking with two empty hands. In this electrification. And within its occupations and opinions."

Where nothing has ever been (payment), I can't say that I can speak where nothing's ever been (the most precise payment) concerning ultimate conditions. That which speaks of glowing conditions: Cement. 'Cement!'

Payment. 'Payment!'

The 'distant' presses in quite close to the 'nearby' and expands it, equalizes it, where nothing has ever been, nothing of these final, ultimate conditions — if I think about it. Where no cellulose has ever been. Of schnapps. Of worker slime. Comintern. Where nothing of misery has ever been.

Do you know who or what is speaking here?

And who is replying?

Do you know who's moving forward from one weeping word to the next without looking around?

Such ideas. Ideas of no particular flower. Of no particular bush. Of no particular bird.

What conditions?

If I think in a more precise way, it was in fact not a precise bush and there were no turning flowers, either. There were circles. And lines. Pain-lines. Geometry. Mosaics. In several honey-colored Chinese dragons, being pulled across a brightly illuminated firmament-cement, but who is pulling, and who is illuminating this thickety bushthicket? The dragons get caught up in 'the poplars'. In 'the mangos'. 'Decision-guinea'. The poplars become the more 'precise decision'. Mangos in which something has been caught. Something with final conditions that are:

Weeping children hanging on the dragon. With four legs and a turning flower. Moveable tails. They have to, they

must accept 'this condition'. They pull, to the very end. They see a shining condition: Forgiveness, cement, mourning.
Yet they do make precise resolutions. They're speaking of 'enormous meadows'.
We're speaking of enormous conditions (flowers). We're speaking about enormous final conditions that we can't fulfill, even if we desperately want to, be it speaking within a fire, be it going into a fire, be it falling into a world-fire that affects all of us. We simply do not reach mechanical systems. We see them and we hear swinging in the distance but we can't reach them. It turns us. It turns us onto our backs. We're afraid. Of what we see, too (payment). Of what we're saying, too (the most precise payment possible). We can't write anything down that we think we recognize, the Selvas, cement, payment, the matrix, we can squelch nothing, we can't make anything believable, we remember nothing, block, and cause nothing to be forgotten, O, we're worn out. We go away.
The flight of a word that's blossoming ends at the edge of an ocean. 'At a blossoming ocean'. I — I am a bridge-end. An earthmover. I come to a tree. To a pear. They're strangers. 'Are they all waiting?' This flight from red revolution ends at this strange ocean. Deceptive strangers. Medusa. Electra. Friends. Little bridges. If — if they allow us to flee. But nothing, nothing is more difficult than that. Letting us flee. If they let us flee through the

weeping Selvas, motionless and still — waiting, motionless, still and waiting, rudder movements nudging in the intervals, nudging toucans (Lenin), and small monkeys. If released, we reach the steadfast ocean at this unchanged exit and close.

But we will not cross it. No, we shall fall in the sand and count: The steadfast ocean (1). The ocean that's disappeared (2). The humanly-inhuman ocean (3). It is the ultimate, final condition. The final, great condition that's been given us. We take the ocean in our hands. Many accede unto it. We are a bridge-end. To an ocean of possibilities, and to conditions, in our hands. 'Are we vermin?' We place it to our lovely mouths and drink it dry. Meaning, we're pulling the steadfast ocean unto us and drinking it dry. Now, we are the final condition. The amalgam.

We shine in this undulating debate.

No one contradicts us in this assuagement.

No one contradicts us as this is the final condition.

If I ever were in a night . . .

No questions (payments, cements).

In a final, generic night that we embrace, I stand up, am presented 'a tree', 'flowers', 'libels', 'Artemis', 'chemistry'; I stand up in this sleepless night and descend with a yellow dragon across a blurring patch of forest that opens and closes itself like a shut-in child with the slightest of worries. He's 'opened'. He closes again. Dead. Paid. I set

the conditions. Nothing is more difficult to do than that.
I, I open the debate. You hand me the smoking lily.
Yet I've *seen* nothing.
How should it continue,
that which rests in the turning flowers
(outermost payment)?

OUT OF THE APPLE GARDEN

for Petra Ganglbauer

I saw her coming out of the apple garden, supported on one arm. I saw her emerge from a comprehending world and saw her fall into a shredding world, falling in every blossoming direction. Into an elder-tree of death, and of shredding. In those blossoming main axes of liquidation, namely: spite and deviation. I saw her go, into that golden stain and that fuel of developments, maladjustments, metamorphoses I saw her go and so I see her now in a final reality (cut), and I fondly recall her new formulation, ensconced within storms of soft metamorphoses, and small metamorphoses (cuts); and she'd been cut by the foxtail, and she'd been cut by a defective woman's foxtail, and everyone is cut by this woman's foxtail and reassembled, anew, and incorrectly named AQUAMARINE according to that steady image of blossoming reality within that finality (cuts).

Vague for blossoming hands, vague for the blossoming eye for which she'd been desired, without mass and momentarily sliced in pieces, and capped, on a canal ship, in a final tranche. Her head with bands, her blossoming

head before that background of an elder's main axes, the axes of a dead man, and of being torn apart, and she'd been sliced away and her hanging tongue, gliding gently to the ground, had been kissed by the words: 'Comedy', 'Ox-', and 'Pascal'. Her tongue was an instrument of appeal. But I lost it. Her head with Pascal bands had been placed in display cases facing the café "El Popular" in the streets of Mexico City, facing cinnamon stars, and modernity, and apple pastry and cinnamon opportunities, all those opportunities, those catastrophic opportunities. I lost her. I could stand up.
Where I had gone. It falls down.
"If it's true that an axis is running away on her end, and if it's equally true that this reality might be able to look back upon a blossoming axis, and that this axis would just happen to be truth on its own sharply approaching axis, and that each has his own axis, each with his own body-axis, and that each has another blossoming axis on his pointed body-end, then, well, you have to ask yourself 'where am I going?'
For you can see everywhere at once, and forever, into blossoming axes, see people walking on a square tableau, on a proscenium, whether with dogs in the gardens of Mexico City, with a jackdaw, arm in arm entwined, laughing, and recognize her," said her head just before it was sawed off.
It had been placed on its right-hand cinnamon cheek yet

had not remained still between various metamorphoses, that is, filled with golden cakes, cold cuts, ads, for it'd wobbled, and I'd taken note of it.

Now, this head is dripping into my blossoming reality.

"The shredding wolf," she says.

In its end, the axis. A melody. Mistakes.

I've commented on that (cuts).

Thing is, she no longer makes ship decks. I told her she ought to go down the axis with me or enter below, down the curve. Just as we do it, every yellow morning.

She'd gone with me, to the very end of her axis. She'd uttered the word 'comedy' and the words 'divine comedy' before I sawed off her head. Her beauty increasing greatly in the devaluation. On a canal ship. Cuts, in final reality.

She no longer makes yellow ship decks and she no longer makes any decks from that wood of the elder; she always made decks from that worn-down wood of the elders in order to break — in order to crash herself through all times and spaces, through killing, and through tearing apart. She'd sold these decks and killed the buyers in doing so. They'd felt her, in dissolution. Along with a yellow collapse.

"Depth would be a blossoming height," she is to have said.

I'd soaped her breasts for hours and used a leather strap in doing so, 'a wire brush', in praxis, but who or what is a wire

brush, supposedly, if one is killing and shredding, for a wire brush is enveloped with fog through this killing, completely enveloped, and in yellow practice it cut heavy breasts from her rump and laid them on my naked knees as I sat. Sometimes, well, I sat on a rock. Mostly I sat on the wood of the elder. I expected a miracle of becoming-form. Her breasts as a cap. As gloves. In the final moment, I sat on a white mark of the elder, in a colorful chair, decorated with bands and banners, and bore an axis-star made from the branches of the elder, bound to my blossoming back that birds and sparrowhawks entered at will, duplicated birds, a martin, a bread-colored fox. As long as I could remember I'd made a star from wood of the thicket and fixed it on my back with intestines. Well, she no longer makes any yellow ship decks and no longer sells them to 'the buyers'.
"On the knees, the horse's blanket.
On the knees 'her attentiveness'," she says.
"Just you think of the horse's blanket when you go with me to the edge of the fountain on the world's axis and are looking within. Into deceptions, loveless, and into storms. A forming-shape. Horse's blanket of deceptions and storms going right across the drawing floor. He left us later."
I laid her caramel-breasts and hail-breasts on a sawmill worker's yellow horse's blanket, where they were blinking, like a cinnamon-pole, a pole of yearning desire and of

shredding apart. I set up everything, quite new, on their poles, and I set up the netted axis, new and timeless, on my back, on its caramel-poles, and I cut it all out, quite new on one, and she said: 'civilization hostile time'. With an even-keeled main axis: illumination and the vertical: order.

I'd gently touched those quivering breasts. And I'd killed her in order to look into her, and I'd seen them coming from the apple garden that I might see into their 'body end departure point' and be able to go in there, loveless, and I enlarged the throat orifice on her rump just wide enough so that I could believe it possible to enter and disappear as a second skin within her body. As a puppet. As an assembler of yellow collapse.

"If we proceed logically, we also proceed attentively into the bush and great landscapes, people and swarming-animals, my attentiveness on naked knees," she says. "As lumber traders, as sawmill workers, in steps of change, everything enlarged, everything split apart and newly glued together so it can be left alone. Everything that knew me."

I enjoyed killing her. I killed her to protect us, to change her, for me, in final desire, she'd be holding everything together, now, she'd be holding all together now in a final act of desire, she would've said: "I'm holding everything together (stipulation), one might say, I'm holding us both together in an ultimate embrace."

She threatened to hit me, gas and cripple, she threatened me with pestilence and amazing arguments under the theme of: 'Phoenix' and 'Ox-' and 'Pascal', and I would've liked to have killed her and I'd have killed her to protect her that we might morph unto one another, and I'd have cooked her and eaten her that I would protect her within me and morph unto me as a complete *desire*, a final *desire*, using the horse's blanket to do it, and the leather soap and my bodkin, and the reamer, the apple garden, along with several gentle acts that are since lost, a blue tool, not coming back, just as well left unsaid, just as well spoken about, and you might say: she's been disenfranchised, and I've disenfranchised myself, and we've escaped from ourselves.

Standing at the yellow window on a morning to observe a blossoming power plant, summed up as: The most distant. "We are killing the whole morning over people, whatever occurs to us, right up to midday, right up to the midday of a final dismemberment, and killing is the poison and killing is the anti-venom, however it happens, and we're killing the whole morning over people so that we might see into them; and what we see is blossoming dust and what we hear is the most distant and what we see are relative choices, radix, and what we hear is people as dolls floating past going to most distant points. We are taking people as dolls in our hands and pulling them over to us. And thus we travel to those most distant points. Bodiless.

Just think of the horse's blanket," she said.

She stood before me in a thin white coat, a tableau in her hands. A flaming proscenium. Framework at the ready. Drawing floor. A flaming library. People with dogs going in there. Sugar taken from her tableau, everything put together there, even a bread-colored fox and a crying mistress, and I'd hit her in the face and hit myself in the face all throughout the yellow morning right up to midday, and she'd said: "Always half a day's time, half a night for you and for me," and I kissed her hanging tongue, and from her blood trickled more blood, and as it was good, I sprinkled some sugar on it, using all the sugar in the whole world on her, sugar ideas, crying women, and I made a thousand-pointed crystal from her, with the sugar, and with the foxtail. The blossoming woman, as fretwork. And the entire time, her hands holding the little tableau. Church steeples shaking in the provinces.

Subsequently, I salted her. She'd been yellow salt of the world. Her nature remaining changeable and tangible. Her nature remaining flickering, and I called her AQUAMARINE and transformed her utterly.

"We'd heard many birds, even the bloodiest, even the most distant, we would've prepared them in the sciences (coma) and released them once more in a time quite hostile to civilizations, we would've heard the storms in the people and the rustling of dolls' clothes and the movements of insects through skirt pleats," she'd have said, "and that happiness would be indescribable and incomprehensible; and I would've been in a state of incomprehensible happiness, of final deviation. Of killing. While all eyes were upon me. While all were closing me shut. In good hands."

"Nothing. Initially. Skirt," he would've said.
"Skirt, more intense.
I want to shout my name. Beyond
inconsolability. Drawn from *numbness*. Beyond
that *galling* counting system. The night we're passing through.
Dictatorial reason. We hear ourselves.
I'll separate myself from the horse's blanket, that of a sawmill worker that would've been buried in a flaming library, in the revolution-library. Weeping people moving there, with jackdaws. Nothing to fear. Because sleep rests within blossoming dawn. And we move toward one another with this utterly consuming idea, we move toward one another with the idea of the revolution. We move toward one another with the burning-idea!"
MARINE says in the café El Popular in Mexico City.
"We hear ourselves, how we get up and are buried, within a counting system, and how Another, a blossoming Other, has come," says MARINE. While we've all been on the axis of this counting system or star system and in the water, too, within Pushkin, and sawing into temporary

wooden bridges and gliding into distant flames. We're putting an end to numbers. Using evenings of long ago that moved as well, using masks from antiquity, full of stars, and plains of it, too."

"We all want this." MARINE stands in the center of the overfull café on a smeared-up star. The exact number of stars is 27. Their system is milky-white, coffee-brown and non-continual in these spaces. It holds a swizzlestick in its hands in the form of an grayling, and it must be a dried out grayling. And quite burdensome. A string fastened to its left eye, swinging it over its head with great velocity. "We all have this yellow desire. For presence. For satiation." The grayling moves through the spaces and washes over faces of passersby. Grayling, passersby. "I know I'm in the water." Their heads clap together behind. They all have a yellow desire for presence. Those who are present — political, and burning. We're told. But down. The revolution begins there. Amply. We're all happy. We all are burnt. We all should be quite happy. We're standing in the flames. The swizzlestick swirls round the political and divides it. And that, too. Middle left. Middle right. Nothing. At first. Skirt. I want to call my name. Outside the system, though. When I'm in the burning library. Of a counting system. Periods and prior and Pepsi. There are sugared periods ('no', 'yes'), and there are unsugared periods, and a dried grayling is moving right straight through each and every blossoming policy. "I know we're

in the water. In a farce." The grayling says nothing to those burning politics of the present, and MARINE says nothing to the burning politics of those present that consists of both schnapps and praise for cardboard houses. MARINE's politics is the swizzlestick. Its color, milky-white and coffee-brown. It rests on every star. A blossoming grayling. Its sound is that of the Atlantic. Its divisions, transcontinental. Its swizzlestick is formed by Brezhnev.
And Stalin's carrot.

"Think about politics.
Think of the horse's blanket.
In adhesion. This question cannot be asked of me. In the consistency of a blossoming grayling." MARINE says to the AQUAMARINE, within periods, standing next to him with a picture of the red revolutionary.

"We can draw a blossoming axis through the revolutionary, best if in red, corpus-red, that returns to the beginning, and we can look into him from all sides but cannot enter," says AQUAMARINE.

"We all have a desire to be 'present'. In the political. In enjoyment," MARINE answers her.

"Presence, unseen. An important contribution. Completely worthless. If we aren't lying. The next. Worthless. We would all be happy in infernal politics, but, well, that's a mess and a piece-of-soap presence. We're told we'd be happy (miserable). But we doubt it.

And we hesitate. We're told we have to clean ourselves up using this piece-of-soap presence. They speak of cleansing. Our bloody hands would be washed with a politics of cleaning-up. We've placed our hands deep inside the red revolutionary in search of this promised presence, and we've submerged our hands in the black revolutionary after we'd opened him right on his sharply arriving bodypoint, and it's there that the world's yellow axis of truth becomes visible. We let the revolutionary trickle from our fingers. Counter-revolutions.

We've been promised an illuminated presence if we wash our hands in the blood of the revolutionary. But they've forgotten that they were already bleeding before. Bled long, long before. And they'd not have allowed us to bleed with a revolutionary. Irrelevant, whether red or black. Now: Those we did not see. It's enough. I know, worthless. They would not have allowed us our presence with that blood of the revolutionary. Not even the smaller one.

Our yellow hands have been bleeding for ages, before presence, in onions, a glass, leopards.

That's enough. We're all happy.

We carry the leopard with us on our backs as a hope, his bite in our pocket as will and idea and from nothing we carry blue splinters of glass in our hands, and the red onions on our tables as hubris of exactitude, and we're happy.

We turn the onions, glass, leopards a degree further, a degree of bleeding from
Hegel-hybrids-doxa
(of a row of birds)
and mild secularization. We've got our illuminated presence in a turned onion; in the turning bite of turned and illuminated leopards," answers MARINE, "it's enough."
   "Think of the presence.
Think of the yellow horse's blanket.
Within and outside a little horse's blanket of presence.
Forget presence that's not within the onions.
Forget presence that's not in the leopards,"
says AQUAMARINE.
"But our presence, for ages, has been our distance, distance from those leopards, and from those onions, distance that cannot be overcome. Politics is an uplifting of this distance. Politics, however, is the apparent presence of the political through the blood of the revolutionary. Bakunin in Novalis. Kropotkin, Zapata, Pepsi.
Revolution, counter-revolution, account. We're distant. In sufficient measure. We will no longer try to understand. That which cannot be understood without disappearing in doing so. We are distant. We must, however, stand outside in order to be present. People, at whatever altitude, at whatever depth, they bring us a new presence, not the illuminated human-presence that we're seeking, not this, and not the one we're seeking in vain, in the distance, not

this, not as will and the imagining of a thousand-headed nothingness and no one, no. No, a new presence, with people glued to one another, their actions in that gluing more manifold, and Bakunin in Novalis, and honey-men that are indistinguishable and indivisible from one another, they do not bring us this new presence that we need, and it is irrelevant whether they are bleeding or not, whether they are slaughtered or not, or whether we saturate our indifferent hands in their blood, categorically, hypothetically, it's just so, people carry nothing away from this, bring nothing back, and add nothing to it. They're not even capable of withdrawing a single speck of dust from the whole thing, or contributing anything to it. We are constantly affected by those things we touch. With the exception of people. We doubt. Then we're free of this presence. We are, however, constantly present and tired of the entirety of a blossoming world in that final moment that's affecting us. I've seen the igniting flame. There, where I began on this happy night.
And I said:
Onion. Glass. Leopards.
Onion (Zapata).
Glass (Kropotkin).
Leopards (Pepsi).
And thus began the deception of politics with a pre-deception of touch.
Onion Zapata.

Glass Kropotkin.
Leopards Pepsi.
Just as we ought to begin this last deception.
We remain present in the flowers, though!" cries MARINE to AQUAMARINE in periods standing next to him along with a picture of the red revolutionary. Where it was. Just as it had been made. In sufficient measure.

I am moving my hands that have been bleeding for ages, in great speed, and I forget them where I was, and yet they continue to move until evening arrives, and they enter it. Pause. Or, hands that really stop. I'm moving my bleeding hands in this storm of a history and turn them, slowly, in time. Blossoming. Their quick, horizontal movements describe: 'the blue morning of the revolution', or 'the red evening of the revolution'. The left one is called MARINE, the right, AQUAMARINE. These hands tell their little story in the rain, and I know nothing more than this little story of my hands unleashing cooling rains, a story of my hands that've been blossoming and bleeding for ages, and passersby tell them, tell small, cooling parts of my story and bring it further along, and it unfolds a collapse and crashing of passersby and of graylings that are wooshing above their amazed faces and moving right through their empty heads, unfolding a yellow collapse of passersby, of pathmen that I see in the blizzard of this history, an extinguishing of yellow

passersby whom I remember in an earlier lemon-colored time. In subsequent time within the yellow collapse of the history. A coincidence that marks ground zero. The ground zero angel. The firmament departure point. Slowly, they've become stars. Their exact number, 27. Slowly we go from one glazed star to another. Bakunin, Novalis, Zaputa. In the café El Popular in Mexico City.
AQUAMARINE screams: "Opened! Opened!" Slowly, yellow stars are forming. And a cinnamon pastry. One that we didn't see. The precise number of this opened, sometimes rhombus-shaped star: 27. It's system, a swarm of rhombuses. And graylings. And opened for those who are moving, those who are crying, and those who are utterly exhausted within the storm of this history. And while I move from one glazed star to another, and I see fire-ships, and I see evenings with ends, and I see evenings without ends but with a lightning corona, and I'm carrying a rhombus-shaped axis network made of wood from the tree on my back, and I call to AQUAMARINE:
"My head needs to be opened! Open this forged head for this history's tiring blizzard, or in the rain — but don't allow me to understand it!"
When I fall face-flat from exhaustion, in yellow disappointment, the axis network assumes the form of a shield on my back, covered with stars. Dogs go there, as do leopards in galvanization, pragmatic. When I fall onto the starry floor, the snow of the history covers me out of

ultimate exhaustion and in yellow disappointment, and MARINE holds my hands while AQUAMARINE sits on my back. She opens my mauve-decorated head with a drill and a black bodkin and drills a circular hole in my crown. She removes a piece of my brain with a wooden spoon. The piece that's responsible for separation, and for the presence. For the political. The monkey-theater. For the Zapatism. Bakunin Pepsi. For presence and effortlessness, the political, the deception-politics, the politics of deception, the politics of pre-deceived presence, of the fleeing, of the bleeding, and of the creation of the furry boot. She removes six pieces of my brain. I've asked her to do so. And I know she likes to do it. While doing so, she hits me lightly on the nick of my neck and my chin bumps the stars.

"If we enter this adorned head, in the final blizzard of history," says AQUAMARINE, "it'll be possible to see these sugared circumstances, and the sugared mechanical idea, and to correct that mechanical idea. We see geometry in these heads, split wide open as they are. A crystal. And we'll insert a black bodkin deep in the head, and in saying and doing that, we really mean the knife of this history. And it'll cut the sugar-crystal. And we'll change the geometry of the history from a triangle to a rhombus. It might be the dragon we're expecting, the one that flies well over the blossoming fields of the history. We'll unfold the little rhombus, covered with yellow paper and juniper berries.

All figures, figures created by people, however they might actually begin, however they happen to end, and it might be late, and it might be early, and they might be standing in flames or wasting away in amber-colored deserts, 'girls with dandelions', whatever, 'chrome', whatever, for all these waiting figures are figures created by lost people (apartheid) in tiredness, in disappointment, in a collapse, with nice cool lines between them," says AQUAMARINE, "and they mean very little, all these blossoming figures, whether juniper or Hermes or the brain that's been drilled into, they've all been created by exhausted people (silos), created by people in disappointment and are thereby utterly worthless. They're present and absent at the same time, are enclosed in solidification and in dissolution at the same time and at the starting-point of my morning discussion. Girls, with dandelions. Nil-nil."

A carter and steel worker are near me, nothing without doubt, and it's begun again — many await his arrival in the apple garden, extra early, but he hasn't heard it yet, he's opening his gluestuck mouth on which something is glittering, habits, assertion, praxis, nil-nil, and it all means that those white barracks belong to the carter and the storm that's falling within it, too. Nil. And belong to the gravel pit, too. Double-nil. To yesterday. And to games of every color. Belong to this, if I should fall out of these white barracks in the rain, if I should fall out of these barracks of an absolute, regulated thought that's also a non-thought, fall into 'neglect', into 'tetra', into 'chaos' and into 'deca'. In this blinding rain. If I know it, too. Worthless. Aghia deca. This light rain as nature's advert. Drink something! Understand, finally! On this history's fountain's edge. Leaning on one arm. Just like an amber-colored dog. Within the little fireworks of this history. So who's being ground up? And who's doing the grinding?

The storm grabs me by the ankles in a state of seclusion, worthlessness, and joy, in the apple garden, very early, in the apple garden along the winding river, rushing, turning, above it a slowly-turning firmament (cement), and the storm grabs me by the ankles and twists me high, for a moment, so that I am able to see past the fountain's edge of the history, throwing me against the door of the black barracks. Wearing a rhombus network on my back. In the hands of a Chinese dragon. In my ears, juniper and grass. Next to me, the tableau. Sugar. Revolution-cutlery. Gas-flags. Dummies, salsa. Flaming people with dogs and jackdaws moving about there, hands white. If I'm able to fly, I'll be level with 'closer stars'. And there, within the barracks' lightless interior, MARINE and AQUAMARINE deal multi-colored cards and throw them on the top of a knee-high table or footstool, shouting. Cards of yellow collapse. Of this storm. Barracks. Of the apple garden. Of the worthless. Of history. Of the carter. Six different cards, 22 exactly alike.

This storm casts me against the carter's barracks door and

it breaks. But the storm is diminishing. Just as the leather of principles shrinks. And the yellow storm grabs me by the ankles, firing me right straight through the barracks and out the back door again, and playing cards spin to the ground, on them variously inscribed 'today', 'rock quarry', 'yesterday', and 'Ravensbrück'. I recall those principles I'm inventing with my hands, principles of utter worthlessness. Or, rather, it's bright in this accumulating rain that I'm touching with my fingers. And the fireworks continue.

The carter is nearby, AQUAMARINE says he's bringing apples through the cinnamon-brown apple garden, out into the ceremonial area. Into the political. He's bringing us away. No one's returning. Nothing's lacking. Naphtha. Ravensbrück. MARINE says the apple cart has driven right across my cinnamon-brown chest and my limbs are now a great distance from one another, yet I can still see the closer stars and the edge of the firmament. On the fountain's edge of history, 'I'm from the apple garden'. On the headstone.

An iron worker or a piranha is near me, AQUAMARINE says he's bringing bloody handguns through the garden, right into the ceremonial area, right into Catholicism. Very early. MARINE says there's an entry wound in my cinnamon-brown chest. Shameless muzzle!

Didn't look down to the water. The carter moves down the river in a stained rowboat, next to him a steaming horse and an amber-colored dog, and he's moving close to the shore, his rudder's caught in willows near the shore, his hands limed and signaling to me.

"Whose imitation," the carter signals.
I answer, screaming, "How speak?
What are you remembering?
What can you signal?"

"The ceremonial area. The collapse," the carter signals. "A carter and an iron worker are near me," the carter signals.

THE TWO-HEADED BREADLADY

Darkness has come and everything has come.
Greeting the darkness.
Greeting the night.
Greeting the Arctic.
A yellow moment of collapse. Light-tower and chance.
I've attained it through this shredding of intermittent distance.
Or, nearly distance: Meadow — creek.
I want to unite everything.
From a biting Arctic in a springtime-like negative.
Bakunin into Novalis.
And back again.
I must collapse everything.
Where did I go after listening, supported on the yellow flower?
And where did I go after speaking, supported on the yellow flower?
'Come' could be a mustard-colored flower.
'Go', a glove.
When I speak, I remain nearby. I distance myself, so that a

prototype of the distance through plant-colored speaking:
Darkness has come and everything has come!
(Greeting darkness)
(Greeting the night)
Last objects and being in this mauve-colored Arctic!
(Greeting the Arctic)
But which one?
That one, of speaking.
Speaking, however, in a lightning-weather asymptote.
If you listen for a long time and are waiting, a weather-machine will begin to speak. Ideal lightning-automation and a thunder-wedge. It might be an animal-machine, too. An apple garden. A child-metaphor. A big schedule for connections. Of all these disasters. The political snout, in the hollyhock.
Nothing, and at the same time, something, within mauve-colored recognition once more.
When will I finally begin to speak in concrete terms?
Out of the concrete. Out of the praxis. Out of the political snout. In a laundromat.
For a holy family. To attain privilege.
It's blinding. But I'm of Mexican heritage. Just out of the apple garden, that's where I've stooped over. I'm speaking, doubled-over. I'm speaking from Oaxaca, Mexico. From a standpoint of parity.
From an elevation.
And thus, from nil — nil. There's absolutely nothing

here, and yet at the same time, mauve colored recognized once more:

'bridge', 'factory', 'boulder',

'red'. Why use slang? Social?

Torture of the working classes?

'Corpus-red' and a recollection of a lost form of transmission: THAT WHICH HAPPENS — FARCE, WHY IT HAPPENS — SYNDICATE, as it *will* happen — through subsequent slumber. Near mauve-colored apples.

Scream-out-sleep: where have they gone!

Where have the politically-murdered gone, and where do they rest now? Or stand, in this screaming-sleep?

Where did I go, after listening?

Many had spoken.

From the political gauche. In the black kitchen. Inquisitory fragments of speech from the apple garden where you doubled-over.

Where did I go after speaking, supported by a foamy creek and a yellow flower? The creek dividing meadows and voices of lovers shouting a wintry scream and shouting of spring-time-like crimes.

I recall the lost, though it remains lost-spoken. Foamy divisions within this story. The mauves. The disasters. The day's intelligence. With its dog. For where do these hands emerge, now, before this face? Suspicious. Damaging. That's what was lacking.

And then — it passes — into the flowers.

I'll remember the lost — but all will remain lost — even in recollection:

It's a yellow age, namely. A question. What a relief. Pauses. Sentences. Mistakes. A crow standing on her little crest and moving about, speaking disjointedly. It's not necessary. In a negative of this story. It's speaking there, in late connection, hearing and speaking at the same time, thus perplexed, thus, seeking aid, meaning in a partial clipping, extinguishing, its been in the background for quite some time, but mute, yet diverted, in front of a rooftop window, there it is, yet leg colored all the same.
A passing breadlady.
First. If you wait.
If you move:
A semi-dark breadlady (mala). Pebbles. In her hesitation of speech. I perceive her in hesitancy, as everything else, too, and it falls away, and it deceives, as everything else, too, though, a paradigm, and a peanut and a fabrication. It remains evening. Distant.
None shall wait.
I'll have to be quick about it. I'm speaking about acceleration; speaking must be accelerated. But from where?
If I wait, she'll surely still be there.
Wait — for what?
For the conclusion. For the mistakes. For the breadlady who brings together part of her lost story, together with

her little loves, to recall, to recall something that could be a part of the lost story AQUAMARINE. In delaying. Waiting, waiting to be forgotten through an acceleration within those extracted sequences in which I'm speaking, aimlessly, touching her and kissing her fleetingly, beneath her leg-colored fur skirt, waiting to remember, to forget, and indeed, staring alone with an endlessly fixed stare, staring at it through that lemon-colored glass of her shop, shrouded in half-darkness.
As an end of complete helplessness. An amalgam. And I see a mauve-colored hand, emergent from her head.
She's sitting on a brown voliere, of course, with 'ideal calorie count'. Attempts. She's sitting in the mauve-colored interior of her shop near groups of workers near the depot, sect. 5, with green and grown-bread opportunities. And what if I touch her. For nothing. And no one. It's a yellow age, actually. Pebbles. Bread-lightning. Bread aberrance, right down to the intestines, uzzis, gloves, shots and ignition gas.
Beneath apple trees where you've doubled-over.
Before a rooftop window. Her voliere, in hesitation at speaking, bowed from wire and outfitted with material in head, in hands, and behind it, error of a face, partially beaten back, level hand supporting her chin. Much like a mauve-colored dog. The conclusion.

Should I see her in yellow. If she should see. If she is seen

and spoken to, and so, lemon-colored, utter penetration from every side, in a half-darkened showroom, sitting on a brown voliere.
"Now it's about sugar-
ideas! Aberrances! The negative!" she cries, "Whatever doesn't melt, shines, reflects, and —
(why can't you say it?)
even if it's penetrated in rash recognition by staring through lemon-colored glass! Climax.
I've overlooked so much. As an utterly worthless passerby. On cobblestones. Most. Most important.
I've diverted suddenly foaming murderers that are connected to tired things through hasty recognition in a mauve-colored landscape. A blue factory of murderers. In as far as I've counted them, those before me. Or flown. Or rushed.
'Creek streams!' 'Rushing waters!'
Most.
I've diverted them by looking forward, just in front of a rooftop-window, and I've brought them far, though it's still evening, and I've pushed them onward until I've said: Blue-clad murderers in a mauve-colored landscape, and thereby having attained absolute parity.
The ultimate equality.
Blue-clad murderers in a mauve-colored landscape.
A complete cancellation.
Nil-nil.

I'm bringing it all there.
I'm bringing it all there, everything that's in front of me. Or behind me. In collapse. Then, I'll have it all set aside, the equivalent of a worthless passerby."

Later then, following restless disappearance of murderers and that chalky-white workers class and swarms of bombers, and when I've finally found a duplicate form of penetration by turning my back — when I turn around, when I hesitantly turn around — I find my way to a duplicate form of penetration, of speaking, of remaining silent, of killing and of telling. Going forward and speaking, looking back and hearing. That double-helix of penetration. At the very last moment. And even if it's only a kind of rule-rendering. I've found a duplicate form of penetration, a transformative shape in that half-darkness, a double-headed breadlady sitting on her brown voliere, with uzzis, turning heads, turning them in penetration of nothingness and of mauve-colored recognition solely by staring into lemon-colored glass. I could stand up. That doesn't belong to a third. In nets. From all sides. It's simple. As a sphinx. In the turning of a head. A yellow moment of collapse. You see, I'm searching for my lesson.

The double-headed breadlady washes the flower covered floor of her store, sitting down. I'd very much love to give it the shape of a plant. The goldenrod of collapse.

Mornings, in yellow. Now other flowers are blooming, in pairs, on: 'The double-headed'
'breadlady is washing'
'sitting on the'
and soon.
Goldenrods. Yellow glass. The blue mixer.
A picture of a beginning and of an end.
A picture of arrival and of departure.
And the noises?
She looks at the opened folding door behind her that leads down the stairs to the basement, and there the geese are collapsing beneath a summoning hand moving back and forth.
She looks to the street rolling downhill and blinking (on waves, in the mountains, in cold forests, but she doesn't hear anything, and she doesn't see anything, and she's accompanying herself in her language, that of very moderate mistakes, like missing words), and she's looking straight into a lemon-colored pane of glass.
MARINE is standing at the door of smeared glass that leads to the street and closes it. Neither peace, nor change. No grassy field. I won't ask any more yellow, blossoming questions, in goldenrods, in a mixer, on a morning in yellow and blue, and he's saying,

"Only darkness = penetration
in the darkness, halfway hopeful, and a fluid landscape
of arrival and departure."

MARINE stands in the doorway holding white bread in a shriveled up left hand that's all cloudy, a weather asymptote, and what is going to happen to me?
Disappear again?
Knowing, that it's cloudy and lightning.
A circular apparition hangs above his left hand with smeary, ball-shaped bread. And it's all very unclear and fails utterly against that concrete, but that selfsame concrete is impressed by words that emerge and follow that blossoming language, yet:
the concrete fails, utterly.
Battered. Wording. Failure. Darkness. Penetration. I've taken heed. MARINE says:
    "Only darkness = penetration
in darkness, halfway hopeful, and overcast voices
of arrival and departure.
A narrow field.
To minimize."

The double-headed breadlady hears a voice singing words in synch. Into the mud.
The geese. The goldenrods.
Parity, again! Elevation. Nil-nil. I'm seeking my yellow lesson. The last mix. Quintessence in fresh tattoos on her arms: 'rabbit-of', 'rabbit'. 'Hand'. 'Weapon'. 'What freedom'. 'Incoherence'. Of final connection. That shines. Of seeing with two different heads, in two opposite

directions. Back to them. To the mistake. Now. Then. Endless deceptions and endless collapse. Greetings to the overcast worker class with American enemies and tattooed enemies of enemies, and she's saying:

"Only darkness —

now, penetration, and waters coursing, slowly, across my closed mouth.

The master. In a milk-glass. In lemon-glass.

A yellow moment."

Darkness has come and everything has come.

A yellow moment of collapse.

AQUAMARINE is standing before a folding door, well, if one thinks about it, that leads to the basement, and locks it. What remains to be said then? Things ought to stay blossoming, and bright. Beneath the flung bodies. In the middle of the room. Then, I, leaning out the window, up in the mountains, in chilly fields, in desolate forests, then getting lost, in both directions at once, double-lost, mauve in my speech.

This, then, as the last one.

A yellow moment, of bees.

AQUAMARINE wears a ball-shaped, painted beehive on her right hand, a beehive that's blurry, and in her left hand that's locked the door, and she's holding a lamp. If (when) she should move in colored steps.

Three animals on her belt, called: 'how', 'then', and 'now'. All these stories about travelers!

Multi-colored, different colored travelers.
Well, as a final stand.

The lamp, recognized anew — the mauve-colored lampion — illuminates the shop space, never mind the lemon-colored light lending decisive distortion to the scene, to that sheer collapse beneath those flung bodies in the middle of the room, taking a final stand.
MARINE moves toward the breadlady bearing white bread who's squatting on the ground as larger and smaller river waves rush in and out, and all around are mountains, and their distant cliffs. The mussel-laden parts of several women are lying next to her. Black ones, and white ones. Hips, and fingers. Returned on the waves. Blurring together. Eels on heels and axles. Morays, questions, in vain. And she's thinking, thinking intercontinentally. Black and white hands resting in her lap, fingers counting, indicating, checking the incomparable, demanding the unreproducible, and suddenly — suddenly a mussel-laden man is there, right there, where there should have been an unreproducible woman — because he'd been slaughtered as a man — to be pieced back together as an unreproducible woman. Women are quite unreproducible. Blue mixers.
A final mix.
A small, bread-colored fox climbing in the hair.
MARINE snaps her in the face three times, bends her

over — backwards — and stretches her out on the floor. He puts the white bread in her lap. Hesitation. A tugboat. The cycle.

A red path? Or was that some other time?

And nothing more to be found?

Master. A yellow moment.

AQUAMARINE comes from the opposite direction, moving toward the breadlady and puts the lamp to the left of her head; she shines the light on her face.

Questions, mistakes, in vain. She puts the beehive down to the right, opens it and throws a rock inside. Yellow droning. Of utter collapse. Of bees and rocks. Of velocity, and silence. Now, and later.

The bees fly right straight through the head of the unconscious breadwoman sprawled across the floor.

AQUAMARINE squats on her, hands on her lower torso. In a final mix. A red path? The cycle? Master. Yellow moment of collapse. The bees leave 'the thousand stings of reality' behind. Impossible to describe them individually. Of 'about two feet'. Thousand heads. Before they disappear. Bee-hydra of reality and of the concrete. That do not exist and never existed, except as a mistake. In river-mud. And in sun-colored flowers. A thousand forgotten glances with a thousand pairs of incomparable eyes.

Saw something.

Something of everything.

At its most urgent. So, the double-headed breadlady gets up, and AQUAMARINE slides back down to the floor with the blue mixer, the body-mixer, and bees cover the face of the breadlady in concentric circles, humming silently, and she speaks in complete equations:
"The bees. The goldenrods.
Nil-nil.
The blue mixer. The yellow moment.
Nil-nil."
Complete elevation as a picture of the beginning and of the ending. As a picture of arrival and of a departure. In sleep, in screamed-out sleep she sets the beginning and the end, the arrival and the departure, in mauve-colored recognition. Slumber falls into itself.

And what happens during this imprisonment?
Within that rushing of large and small waves?
Words and small encounters.
Triple questions, never asked.
Or quietly asked.

Then — this complete equation of speaking succeeds with the appearance of the head moving in MARINE's direction, slowly, and of another head in a second, opposite direction, moving toward AQUAMARINE, coming with lamp and beehive in hand. The breadlady is twice lost in this yellow moment of collapse, and talks about it.

Whatever is seen is screwed down tight, seen twice and rises. A tugboat. A cycle. Red path of elevation.

She'd been in the yellow-tinged Bakunin, according to the breadlady whose lower body has been sheared open utterly and from whom is now flowing fluid of a corpus-red, and thus, our meter-long worker class of the body: A METAMORPHOSIS FOR THE BETTER. Her carbide forehead wills it to be so. In a coal mine. In a dead-silent breadfactory.
Now she's standing across from the cantina. A return to the concrete. But she's of supposed Mexican heritage, evenly divided between Bakunin and Novalis, equidistant, and when she travels, she travels through big cities and landscapes supported on a yellow, sun-shaped flower, supported by a foamy meadow's creek. She's supposedly lived as a little lover in a red cantina that's long since gone, mauve-colored, one that's been neutralized within a yellow-tinged Bakunin and yet equally so within a yellow-tinged Novalis, and you could have seen her from the green hills surrounding the city of Oaxaca. From the goldenrods. In one of those yellow moments. Hesitation, and slight forestalling of her speaking recalling a part of the long-lost story AQUAMARINE — recalled and forgotten just as quickly again.

Her mother was killed in the red cantina of Oaxaca that's

long since gone — killed by those goldenrods — killed through ideal turns of her little head on its very own axis. She could see in all known directions — in her sleep, no less.

In a screamed-out sleep.

Right into the river-mud.

Those murderers would have read loudly from Bakunin and from Trotsky's memoirs as well. The carbide-forehead would have willed it to have been so.

In a dead-quiet cantina.

And from that breadlady's forehead would have grown two heads, if you think about it, one looking ahead, the other looking back. And she could have seen to the beginning and to the very end, and she would have been able to see the future and the departure. She'd have been mauve-colored in her loss of experience. Her mother would've sat in the middle of the red cantina on a ground of rusted loam, and she'd have carried the northern climate in her head and the southern in her lap.

No other adventures?

If truth be told.

Told, until it disappears.

One would've turned her head seven times on its own axis, hit her, thrown her down, her child would've been inserted in her opened lower torso and stepped on.

Nothing more?

The child wouldn't have suffocated or drowned — although it would've been unconscious for some time; kind treatment would have duplicated her.
Multiplied in a screamed-out sleep.
And she would've become the two-headed breadlady. She would've both spoken quietly and shouted in screamed-out sleep. She would've had two distances within her — a north and a south pole distance, a northern and southern climate, a northern and southern Arctic. Of speech.
Bakunin and Novalis. Duplication.
Heated, there.
But for now, she is powerful, and quiet.

Later, she departs — vacant of those yellow signs of extracted power.
In a yellow moment of collapse.
A yellow star.
See, she rules with mafia-parts, with building-lions, with dogs. She kills, to show. She brings the city of Oaxaca under her mild and quiet dominion through the horror of her desire. Desire to reach the forest. Indifferent. A single valid moment.
She desires and is desire, mirror-backward. In a reflection. Heated, there. She's desired all men and beat them, too, she's desired all kind women and kicked them, too, and she would've risen within that yellow-tinged Novalis and it would've been her task to transform

everything to everything, and to mix it, and to transform it back again. And, of course, in addition to that, a blue mixer. A final mix. Quintessence. She'd have had the task and in that she'd have been absolutely sure of creating a new, second Nature, in a reflection. What a relief.

I could just see her hands now. She would've killed all women, sliced them up, dried them and put them back together as fish slops, cord, chiffon. And all her plant-colored children as well. She would've ruled over fiery men through her desire and through those horrors of her girlish striving. She would've hired them to murder all the inhabitants of the city of Oaxaca, that is, to slaughter them, to cut them up and new, mirror-backward, put them all back together again in a lemon-colored reflection. On stiff fingers, and lips of an older woman. She would've forced them to kill, boil and eat leg-colored trash-women and U-kids. She would've done that with the mixer. The blue mixer. The body-mixer. In her lower torso.

Two screws of a quiet ship.

Now she's traveling with yellow signs of attained power.

A yellow star. On her chest.

A yellow moment of collapse.

A cooling.

She's crossing through the city with a dragnet, this gentle, quiet woman, and whomever she encounters, she kisses. She places a leg-colored hand on his shoulder, then his hips, and surrenders killing unto him. Her mafia and

lions kill, that they might show. The double-headed kills, that she might tell. Telling is killing. A cooling. In minimizing. In duplication of speaking and of killing. Showing and speaking.
Or am I forgetting it?
And what do the others see?

A yellow and blue morning.
The master:
A yellow moment.
She's encountered a yellow-clad man, very early, and he's sand-colored and old. What hope! What hope! He's carried a large number of long, sand-colored loaves between his left arm and his body. Under the right,
'a cap of a yellow moment'.
She's stopped him with a quiet word. She's extended her leg-colored arm and placed her left palm on his chest; she's kissed him but only in passing, placing her right, mauve-colored hand on his shoulder, then placing the other on his hip — saying quietly:
"This depiction of a breadseller — this image with its great reflection — it's a yellow star. Yellow sand on the surface of this star. Of the star, of the collapse. Of every hope. I've wished it to be so. Drawn from gentleness and from every effort. But then — I didn't see — I didn't see it.
Didn't see those drifting of sands from one distant pole to the other. The quiet noiselessness of gently moving sands.

And missing answers.
And if there are answers, we can't detect them.
The opaque. A yellow moment.
Circular movements of a dead man, circular movements, star displacements in their abandoned shoes. Their mauve-colored shoes abandoned, but moving, there. Moving, in those abandoned shoes of a dying breadseller. Right into the river-mud.
The vertical and the horizontal, seeing and speaking. Seeing and telling. Into the negative, of this yellow moment. Into the negative of sand-colored storytelling, strewn in all directions."
She's closed her eyes and — for a moment — killed the breadseller. The handle of the knife broken away. The mistake-knife. That's my life. Who understands it?
It's difficult.
Who wants to know it?
A yellow moment. A master.
A yellow lesson.
Since this time, she's lived in the abandoned breadseller's shop next to the worker's depot, sect. 5. She's never left the shop, never again. A shop that hid everything away. As had been said. Now what? Now she's called the double-headed breadlady and will remain precisely that. In both the vertical, and in the horizontal.
Remembering, and forgetting at the same time, a small part of this long-lost river story called AQUAMARINE.

The pillows, sandy, too. Mauve in word.
A mild head —.
Everything — true.
All of these things — she knows.

THE BATH OF LITTLE LOVERS

for Devi Tripur Bhairavi
for Devi Chinnamasta

Nothing has been said about the great stories, almost as if they should remain lost tales, locked in our arms.

Locked in, as lost tales.

MARINE.

And by extension:

AQUAMARINE.

Why describe more than that?

Beginning with a small question. The brake: 'Nor turn away his only light. Halfway hopeful, an exit for these questions'.

Show the entirety. Ask about particulars. Again, the entirety.

Threefold questions, not put. Quietly put.

From this, the cross:

La Cantina de Chichicastnango, Guatemala.

The bright has been uttered. 'Its roof is snow-covered'. Its. Our. Simple question, but to what, past. A dissonant sound, past. 'Into the mud'. Pulling those of the space along, in a majority. 'Quartz. Flint. Light-dark'. Her voliere holds back flowers and geese. It needs to. Her

foyer is without contradiction, yet covered with contradictions, sewn together with the blood of birds, I know it. Thus, obscured, I don't know. Those waiting there say:
"Painting is always an act of obscuring; speaking, always a kind of dissonance,"
and the blue-clad are waiting, engineers (sleep), distance-workers (better), condensing-workers (the gray), shining reflectors of big machines. They also say:
"Should I go under the bridge?
Should I look to see that moving matter underneath the bridge?
Should I myself be a moving space within a static human-landscape?"
The interior of the cantina is overcrowded. With blue-clad drinkers. Bone-breakers. Unto an enchantment of this truth. Unto torture. Its interior, a steam-heart. Its contorted interior serving as an arena for a cockfight. Then, passing over. Or a dogfight. To open up. If it's been made for that small head, that head, not made to be opened. As a tableau for all those stories — for all that are lost — and all that are remembered. The human struggle. The human dismemberment.
There, that lemon-colored interior slice of these things appears. It's a bleeding thing. Whether animal or man. Bleeding, in dismemberment. As a glove covering those things most internal. Brakes, the only illumination. Then, passing. Or, passing — as a bleeding hand, or hand-

essence — on the surface of some lemon-colored glove. Why describe more than that?

Diagonally, across the way, within the interior of the cantina there appears:

The bath of little lovers.

On a glove.

The bright one.

The bath of little lovers is visible, right in front of everyone's eyes, and yet at the same time intangible like those drunks' mutedly illuminated bread factory across from the cantina whose history is quite the catastrophe — with those men of the lake and extended attentiveness present within bodies of fish — bodies that are always present, even if only in the background.

Moving past, just there.

Intangible, following a terror cutting across this little picture before everyone's eyes. Before your very eyes. Terror, cutting away from itself. Moving zones of terror through a static human-landscape.

An extended attentiveness pervades the scene. Nothing is forced. Nothing is left unsaid. But, rather, milled. Milled away, the understandable, right along with the incomprehensible. And vice-versa.

The bath itself will be incomprehensible and only visible with great effort, should it pass, and what can actually be seen, well, that's the question, and what will be seen after that bath passes.

A question, not asked.
Or quietly asked. Fever. Mutation. The collapse of the little lovers' bath. Following the collapse, it'll be spoken about. In as far as is possible. Hearing and speaking. In as far as it succeeds, it's spoken about. A constant change from hearing to speaking and a rapid intersecting following the terror.

The softly illuminated bread factory of the inebriated.
I could say it's an expansion to the rear, in a windbreak, in a row of ball-shaped hills that encompass the evening city, on a zebra-colored evening, a shot in the distance, a denial of the revolution, the positing of a filthy story, and often I feel myself sitting, halfway-hopeful before a creeping brightness. Or, hollow in a second, more precise language in sequence of: The bath of little lovers.
On the left side of the cantina I say: "The softly illuminated bread factory of the inebriated, or the celebratory, whatever you wish, is passing.
So that you'll close your eyes.
Those there, those are shackles.
With their lamps."
On the right side: "The bath of little lovers.
No boulders. No animals. Just the facts."
Both cries act like a beginning and an end to each other. Answer and question. Or, vice-versa. I enunciate them. Or, if you like, it's the lovers themselves that are speaking.

Whatever you prefer. That one, there, that'd be me, if it stayed like that.

The dissolved bread factory of the celebratory is left over from a lost outcry. Thrown together, together with bread and fish in every imaginable color. In front of the bath, perhaps uttered by the lovers themselves, whatever you like. Outcries, thrown about. They drying, in that hair of companionship.

'Bread'. 'Fish'. 'Factories'. 'About'.

'Screwed-up fish'. 'A flapping about'. 'Burned-out factories.' 'Smoking bread'.

Of which the outcry that feeds the bath of the little lovers consists, when it moves ever so slowly, and when it sleeps. But it's not important to state what's happened.

Or might happen.

A double-edged question, not posed. Or posed quietly.

In the absence of connection. And of a final connection.

In zebra-colored darkness. Diagonally, through striped darkness, in the shape of a cantina.

When it's happened.

The supposed questions.

When and why.

The supposed answers.

Light-tower and chance.

The entirety. The individual. The diagonal. The terror. If this diagonal in the shape of a cantina is endured for a long time, terror disappears and 'shining' appears. But it's not brightness, with its lamps. No, it's a story that electrifies. It's like sludge. The human-revolution. I never would've been able to endure such a thing. Uplifted and visible, within human battles, within head rituals, lovers' humiliations (compatriots) in the cantina at Chichicastenango.

It's like sludge. A collapse, that passes. Within wordlessness, beaming, enveloping the bathing scene, and encompassing it, a little wordlessness, that is just as lost as that which is retained, and begins with a cleansing bath of little lovers in a foamy meadow-creek at its feet and shallow end; obliteration of a wooden or sounded display. Obliteration of an animal image, of a bird (into the river-mud), of a bird idol. Depiction of an angel. Depiction of a foaming fish. Of a cantina. Along an alder-lined meadow-creek, that of the celebrating, or gently illuminated fish in that bread factory of the inebriated — now quite far away — and it's all like sludge, and those men of the lake and of extended attentiveness within fish bodies are united over that glittering moment. A lemon-colored glittering of that chain of lights — extended from the dark shore of the foamy meadow-creek to a second, smaller, distant one. A weaker one. Beneath it all, the ship-of-fire.

A glittering of the unfocused in a slovenly-figured landscape, a space, or a half-opened one, meaning an open-standing circus-space in that city of the evening within a landscape littered with people, with people as listeners and as speakers, lions of hearing and speaking, jugglers of focused, unfocused, focuses, past. Those things fallen to the ground called: Quartz, flint, bright-dark. On that human-littered plain before the city diagonal. We're speaking, as lions. Speaking — to the slime of human-revolution. Half-opened and half-shut. Colored yellow. Then, the lamps. One part of the head in the present, a present of speaking, the other in the past. Dead, and living. A glittering of the unfocused that illuminates the interior of the cantina.

The unfocused equalling of the precision of events.

The meadow-creek parallels the cantina and separates it from the bread factory of the inebriated. Or, the celebratory. It parallels the cantina on the front side, as well as on the back side, too, appearing multi-colored, and fixed, and of a brand-new style. As a fleeing word, and as a picture of running events.

Between an endless chain of lights — right before our eyes — hang bodies of figures, needed, of dolls, shrieking, of wind-games, wax, of puzzles. No animals, no boulders, just yellow facts.

My view moving in that span describing the foamy meadow-creek in its undetermined length, then ahead, and back, convulsive, and within it, continuance upward and downward up to the word-fish and in utter obliteration of that intermittent distance.

These word-fish remain in a dull, fixed state.
In the overcast cloudiness of the meadow-creek. With bedsheets from the cantina.
With a little question. And a little answer.
In the stopping diagonal of the cantina.
The word-fish rush along.
Nothing remains behind.

The little chain of lights from which, now and again, one of the figures breaks free — these are lemon-colored, firstly pitching, then releasing against its temple, following pressure from brightly colored, heavily shaped human-revolution to the slime — and its slumber, encased in brightly colored bands, shakes. Before the master. 'The'. The slime.
Figures collapse following the pressure of being shaped. It's the pressure, always. Into the slime. Then, passing. They collapse, from a string of pearls, of calmness. With little lights. Lampions. Non-distinctiveness. Lemon-colored. They smell like mercury. Unscented. Whatever you like. They're inhaling butane gas. They're being formed against their will. They're sleeping a sleep of forgetting. A sleep of suppression. A sleep of subjugation. They're collapsing into mauve-colored depths, or mauve-darkness, as you wish, finding collision, rebound and diminishment of their components. They are collapsing into the foamy meadow-stream. In a stream of metamorphosis. Landing,

sleeping, in a meadow-stream of metamorphosis and leaving it again, sleeping. After a cleansing bath. Remaining asleep until their premature end.

The lights of the small chain of lights shiver.

The first of the two figures, two little lovers that are sleeping or moving around despairingly in a darkness that is quite explainable yet remains unexplained, collapse following the pressure of metamorphosis. There are shackles. Past.

The answer is: metamorphosis.

And, also, the question.

Metamorphosis stumbles close to elimination and they collapse. Into a meadow-stream at their yellowy feet: a flowing stream of deceptions, imitations, and of changing connections, of lack of connection at the same time, of lack of connections between these bodies of little lovers, nicely decorated with colorful bands. Lights from the small chain of lights, as well as those of the ship-of-fire, illuminate and slowly diminish enveloping the bath of the little lovers with good cheer. And the voice vainly searching around them. A master of slime.

Now one can see them in the interior of the cantina, see how they're doing little of importance. They alternately call:

"No dust!"

"No time!"

"No purpose!"

They nourish themselves from an unheard melody.
Without dust, without time, without blades of purpose sticking in their sheared heads, and foaming–up meadow-streams in a red, corpus-red, and shivering little lights forging the sequence.
To this, I might say:
"Meadow-streams are flowing in their heads and the bird of the house is not within.
Yet you're forgetting: the shackles.
Of the master. 'The'. The metamorphosis, the advice."
This new sequence doesn't touch the world of appearances.
It is representation, and melody.
The shivering rhythm of forgery.
In which they speak when those shivering lights illuminate them, and the ship-of-fire.
The word-fish rush along.
Nothing remains behind.

In each and every of these moments outside of time — without purpose and without dust — the lovers replace blades and insert them into each others' heads, hands, feet. Exchanging the ability to keep quiet, to speak, exchanging a type of straining between them, of word-straining, angelic-straining; exchanging beatings, above and beyond, an exchange of word-beatings and angelic-beatings above and beyond.

And in this way they attain a success in imitating the excellent suppleness of nature. A suppleness that completes the exchange, without pain. The metamorphosis. A gliding. Everything washed away. Wooshed. Held, in a moment. A day without purpose. An evening without time. An evening, without dust, a bright-dark striped night. A bright-dark question. A question-night.
Blue-clad drinkers, engineers (sleep), reflectors of steel bridges and diggers, blue grippers, all observing the two lovers, just as amazed as the bone-breakers. There's laughing. A blue-clad master of torture comes forward — and then retreats. His steel band communicates with the lovers in different colors, in a graded system, corpus-red, violet, black, darkening the room. It darkens the room that continues into distant, sharp-pointed hills and into striped hill-movements encompassing the city of the evening — and the city diagonal, too.
It darkens the space, in a Flemish panel style.
The master of torture blows on his bone-pipes. From wing-bones, comes a goose. What else? Judgments, comparisons. It passes. He calls:
"Should I go under the bridge?
Should I go under that metamorphosis-bridge, crossing the metamorphosis-stream, that sees those making all this real?
Should I go under the bridge that issues shining names?
But then. Crackling. Past. To soothe.

Should I, myself, be a moving zone of terror
in a static human-landscape, with beatings?
To soothe 'the light'.
How will human nature ever move and breathe — without me?
And how else can people return to the bridge, the rat, the boulder, the red — and forget the humanlike — but through me?
It's like sludge. It's the shackles. The facts. Of their master."
There's laughing. Jumping, back and forth. Dance steps are introduced and withdrawn again. The rhythm, unknown. The little lovers sit facing each other in a vat, filled to their necks in boiling water. They display a common heart of steam, facing outward. Their throats, extended. Stretched to the roof of the room. Set-up, with cables, lackadaisically. Veins on their throats opened as well as the joints of their hands — and their thighs, too. The vat, or, basin, is standing in the center of the cantina, without reason. There, where a dog is mulling about, and a blue bird, too.
The cantina of Chichicastenango is overcrowded with drinkers clad in blue. And those from the blue factory of bone breakers. The basin represents a wooden idol, a bird idol. If you wait long enough. In yellowy slime. And before you, four arms moving in every direction, and four outstretched necks, blood is dripping from their bills.

Sow-intestines. Stuff. Steam. Severe screams, scream-factories. A small fly emerges buzzing from the dark, in the striped cantina background, if my sweating back happens to brush the voliere — and jumps — within the impression of the basin. So it shall come to pass — on a desert day (extinguishing) — returning to its master.

A beating of wings. 'Beating of wings'. Imprecise swimming movements on the surface of boiling water. 'Imprecise swimming movements', diving movements. There's laughing. 'There's laughing'? 'There's laughing'. The air and movements hold still, shut tight, wave-shaped, striped and obscuring the view of the observer. 'Obscuring'! Flemish painting. Vermeer in the desert. Master of this desert day. Flemish geese.

The two lovers — they had names.

False names. Next-names. Closing-names.

I'll state them quickly.

Why describe more than that?

If it passes.

Love remains, dully fixed.

No little lovers hurry along.

Little remains behind.

The cantina of Chichicastenango houses the bath of these little lovers, in dull fixation.

MARINE!

And by extension:

AQUAMARINE!
Quick, successive names.
Inquire as to the particulars. Show the whole.
Out of this, the diagonal. That's kept out until pain disappears. And until shining appears. And the word-angel. And the fall of that angel.
Two lovers exchange blades that are inserted into their opened bodies, heads, hands, and feet. Comparisons. Judgments. Past. They also exchange words and variable fish, given to each other as gifts, word-angels and fish-angels, play-words arising when blades are used in order to be near one another. Toothy, filthy-purpose and time-rigid blades driving greater language away, greater words, falsified clarity, falsified visibility of figures and, so that I know what they're doing and what's happening, to be completely silent about the reasons and the bright-dark rhythm of reasons, and a yellow rhythm, there, and the master's pulse (for slime), for I don't know what's happening and we don't know why, (it's sludge), and even if we make a desperate effort for a level system of collapse by summoning brightness, we are set, after putting out the lamps, and after a failed attempt at electrification of the light, we are set square to the facts, facts that open, and close, and when opened, figures appear, and then it's closed again, and they fall back (these are shackles), and I don't know what's happening and simplification, that is, the leveling, explains nothing and fails to bring me a little bit

closer in this minor knowledge to that which I seek — to what I'm seeking before I disappear, utterly. When the illuminated cantina will fade through shivering lights into another little chain of lights. Toothy blades driving the forged size of words backward, their blind static, their withered strengths, withered sequences.
Without purpose. Without time. Without dust.
Toothy blades awaken the happiness in both of the lovers, the meekness, the little particularization itself in a passing of handles.
They utter their final statements. They say:
"A boiled hand must always be close to the dust. 'Boiled hand'.
There now — it is neutral, and transformed. Transformed — in a hand of nature. In hand-essence, in this moveable river-hand, flowing beneath large, neutral bridges.
In this hand — holding revolution-cutlery — and shaping the slime."
Statements of love.
And not once is a solitary word possible, for with every final word, a second, smaller one always accompanies it. Beneath skin and bones. A sound of clothes wash. Who's speaking? Past. A solitary word — obscuring to all, to the very end. Installments.
MARINE and AQUAMARINE exchange body parts. Boiled leg, crackling hair, boiled leg and a hundred possible replacements and transgressions against the word-angels

'leg' and 'hair' in a language that I've forgotten as final payment, as a note of yellow collapse right past the language, an odor of gas, blasting caps, whole heads, split heads, gas smell within the language, in asphalt.

MARINE says:
"I speak in partial sentences that don't explain a thing, turning to bleeding backs of the mafia, blue-clad mafia-parts that explain nothing, even when killing, and killing explains nothing — yet it reveals all — and so in doing all this, I'm speaking with the universal-mafia of Chiapas, and I'm speaking with the universal-dogs of Guernavaca. Speaking to them about our split heads. About minimal flight. Fleeing from my head into yours, quite early in the morning.
Once there, dividing myself up into dark and bright halves.
In a bright-dark night.
The universal-mafia of Chiapas controlling the details.
Of this boiled story.
Lightning of thumbs in boiling quintessence.
Twists of the thumbs. Turns of the knives.
Metamorphosis of thumb-piece into knife-piece and right back again. This story, boiled in yellow collapse, in comparisons, in judgments, in facts, and right back again.
Before a
quivering voice coming from a wide-open

mouth. Blinking of boiled thumbs, in assortment.
We agree about this thriving business;
Blossoming profits!
We agree on few friends. Admissions.
Possible questions. Possible answers. Devastations.
Metamorphosis of friends into the boiling.
Few friends!
I insure myself with the assistance of capos, dressed, like me, in blue.
Yet even they are not enough. That certainty, that precision, that 'outermost' that I'm looking for, it's missing. It's passing. It goes past quickly, past — it's a scream, an endlessly restrained scream — from great heights — and everything comes from screaming and everything is made of screaming.
Precision?
It's missing.
Blond, in a night-full-of-questions.
And in release from this imprecise reality.
I've few friends left.
Admission:
They're helping me with the screaming.
In metamorphosis.
We split friends. We extract their meekness. Their meaningful happiness. They crash. They spray. We sacrifice them in the light-dark night. The questioning night. The light-dark goddess within this nighttime-question. That

doesn't exist. The scream-goddess. A goddess within devastation — leg-colored, driving a car (and with a filthy snout too) that answers the boiled indecisiveness of people — asking questions that burn crime and mutations of crime. Of magical truth.
We are going quite beyond friends.
We see them pass by and slowly disappear. We're simply going above and beyond them!"

    AQUAMARINE answers:
"We're beginning with the head exchange. Word-angel exchange. With heads on stakes that speak the word: 'swaying' to each other. Appretur. But strewn
yet swaying nature
flies like a lead-
stranger, oh yes, a confidante, no, a double-confidante in an alien-trusting way that remains indistiguishable
and hidden
as a seductive metamorphosizing one,
a digit, an endless-digit,
a blue-box of nothing
and of mauve-colored recognized
'boulder' 'red' 'colorful glass'
through my head. Past. In this story's subsiding power of vision. Each completing dissection, utterly, just like awful torture unleashing goodness of the shivering. The boiled are ample, and small.

Their stench remains.

And the words that pass by, as you wish, lazily formed but, just the facts, passing into the slime."

The cantina of Chichicastenango is filled at night as a possibility of metamorphosis.
Unto dissection.
Unto killing.
Utter completion?

The turning of
MARINE
to
AQUAMARINE
is a movement of outstretched throats into the Lost. A task. Of the master. It is mild, colorful, appropriately shaped and comes with blowing winds. A human-revolution, driving us. There are shackles. Within these Lost, an elder-lined stream begins. In it, the Lost, the driven ones, blue companies, quartz (Kropotkin), non-quartz (anti-Kropotkin), they're moving easily beneath that metamorphosis bridge, right under and past. Blossoming parts. Anti-parts. A cantina. A cantina that's forgotten.
The Lost are the blossoming forgotten and the little-forgotten constitute the beginning of the cantina of Chichicastenango.
Or, the twisting in which this story finds itself — if you so

wish — that's a movement of throats, bound to the floor with little lovers' wires, there, on the floor of the cantina — throats that remain still and blinking, and they're poles, bright-dark poles, glistening poles of an arctic of speaking in which the cantina emerges — and from which it emerges — and all that remains is the bath of little lovers, the bath of a Greenland of little lovers, and an appendix to the lost story called AQUAMARINE being discussed on a polar cap.

A swaying, black metamorphosis-cap.

Mexican forests. No animals, no boulders — just the facts. There's only terror and slaughter wherever we look. The totalitarian, in a symmetric silence. Then. The neck. Of a white, shooting person. A honey-colored pistolero. Everything is painless. Before the master. An end to bright questions. These poles are blinking in my clothes. Bright-dark poles of speaking. Heads of the lovers. Quartz needles and pinheads in the fishbone of this lost story called AQUAMARINE.

The cantina is a timeless polar cap in a zebra-colored night. In the bright-darkness. Of questions. Of answers. Of reasons. Of counter-reasons. The tale where it all passes us by. The counter-story as it emerges. And just as quickly, disappears. If you wait long enough. In this honey-landscape. With criminals. 'Just as with criminals'. Past. Near the cap, of the cantina, before which I'm now standing in blue, the story passing us by, supported on a

yellow flower, my head wrapped with a white shroud; on my face, a wooden mask depicting a fleeing goose, 'goose', and from its opened beak, blood drips, emptying out of a narrow river. Or narrow stream. Pass. Still unaccompanied by theses. Revolutionary-papers. Restrictions. Appretur. Insults. Fug. Unaccompanied by added-value. Almost, golden soup-eyes. Mexican variations. Profit-eyes. Eyes as political reflectors.
I'm driving a car.
How do I know that?
Into the slime.
I'm driving a car into the innermost realms of human-revolution, there's terror and slaughter wherever I look, symmetries that are of no use to anyone, bleeding symmetries, soon into a belly, soon onto the higher-situated heads, I can't hear a thing they're saying, I can't understand them, and I'm driving a car, how, I don't know. Into the slime. Into the slime of the stream that begins and foams up at the feet of the little lovers. Lined with elders. Clods of soil rolling before their mouths, white balls, reflectors of an arctic of the body, and of speaking.
I'm mild. Colorful. Appropriately formed, dressed.
I'm standing, supported on a yellow flower, my other hand holding a suitcase that jumps open wide, human parts of partial metamorphoses falling to the ground and smoking, and they're improving, and I'm speaking as somebody from a timeless, purpose-less, pollution-less cap speaks:

"It shall look like a sprinkled flower growing in damp stream-meadows.
It is springtime now.
Later, it will look as if it is splintered.
Then, well, it's become winter, quite late.
I throw the opened suitcase from the one hand and the hairy stem of the extended yellow flower far from me with the other.
Then, I lie on my back. The little plate, the little zebra. In bitter cress. With the airiness of pack-string wound around this metamorphosis-nature. Fixed with injections. Crystallized flower touching my goose-jowl, and the quartz (Kropotkin), and the non-quartz (anti-Kropotkin), touching it in a shabbily formed and well-defined winter. Passing.
I balance the cutlery of human-revolution.
'Nil, balcony of speaking, dynamite of the story'. Shabbily formed. Orientation is difficult. The selection sucks. Then, it gets damp. And goes past. And this bath of little lovers ends in winter. In a pole-winter of flowers and dampening bodies. I'm telling the lost story AQUAMARINE from both poles at the same time, from the southern and northern climates of words that pass by in a shivering, splintering arctic springtime. When the ice thaws, the lovers become foamy, lined with elder trees. As it grows around them, they move back into quintessence.
There, they are not visible.

And this lost story AQUAMARINE is not visible when it freezes.
That can be said.
Before the master. Into the slime.
Blinking. Extinguished.
Thawing. Freezing.
Speaking. Mute.
The endless back and forth of speaking in this bright-dark night."

The cantina of Chichicastenango is entered at night as a possibility of metamorphosis.
In blossoming human-revolution.
With mauve-colored revolution-cutlery.
Unto dissection.
Unto killing.
Unto completion.
Before the yellow master.
Unto metamorphosis from a mildly illuminated detail, in a passing whole and right back again.
In the diagonal.
In a diagonal that is also a diagonal of the names of these little lovers:
MARINE — AQUAMARINE.

In a zebra-colored night — within truth-torture — in which torture is accompanied by a snow man. Unto completion. As an improvement. As you wish. It's called this. because of its sudden appearance in this timeless winter, in this zebra-winter, in this winter of bodies. Winter of bodies in which the torture of a snow-woman is manifest, and she's called that because she is carrying two raw sex organs in front of her along with several reflector-breasts in a rusted-out snow-filled pan. She displays them. They're very small. They're smoking. She's driving a car. Both fall to the earth, several times, together with the shining and reflecting breasts and the snow-filled pan, twisted in the snow. There, where a dog is moving about, along with a pig and a chicken. There where those little parts may have been before they were twisted and rent, and now becoming visible, the bright-dark handles of several combs emergent. See, they can be turned on their axis. In all directions. They're moved once to the past and often into the future. When standing still, that is — when the snow-man and the snow-woman disappear in an arctic blizzard of storytelling — so that the story stands still and can be told. Whether in winter, or spring.

The lovers with combs whose leg-colored handles are greased mutter initial, kind words to one another. They remain carelessly formed.

'Hacer'. 'Poder'. 'Quiero'.

'Marroqui'.

The combination in which these words are spoken remains unknown.

And in this zebra-colored night that's accompanied by the torture of the snow-man and the snow-woman, we see — we see that they're wearing snowtires on their feet — bundles of wood on bowed backs arranged diagonally in a persistent diagonal of balance, and the first discussion of the little lovers of Chichicastenango begins from burning tires bound around their throats. Bound, in magical truth. Out of the hollyhocks. Bound within torture, and at the same time, unleashed from it.
Before the master. And into the slime.

MARINE:
"I'm speaking to you about swaying nature — right up to the bird — quite visible within our hemorrhaging.
In every bleeding person, you can see a little bird and a funnel of dust.
A multilingual dust-idol. Anti-speech bird-idol. American bird. Russian bird. Bird orthodox. Bird profit and animation and marked parts of its collapse. Mexican variation. The bird of human-revolution moving about on little legs amongst larger, dying ones. An Arab mosaic displaying claws.
Rhombuses. Crystals. Details of a hidden script:
You're a white dot:
A quartz. A piece of dust.
To live there?
Domestic-crystal? Foreign-crystal?

And:
You'll be nothing more than a white dot. In an arctic landscape. If you should stop speaking. The last guess. In that final, remaining moment. Past.
That you've lost yourself as
hollyhock, hollyhock —
hand stretched out into sprinkled dust, opened again and a then, emergent, secondhand, within that moment of creation. Of the story.
Until this moment's arrived — those things you've said — they're just a word game
within a flurry of words!
These turns are offered to sad dying people as a curtain, as flag of ground-zero, as a winter-hypothesis of the shining revolutionary, right into the slime."

AQUAMARINE:
"Do you remember that forged sequence?
Meadow brooks coursing in their heads — the bird of the house not there?
Past. Into the imprecise. Into the undulating. We're going beneath a bridge vaulting across a foamy meadow stream; we see those that are driving this story. We ourselves, we're driving it all. We can forget those things human-like. We'll crash into mauve-colored depths. Into:
The red. Into a boulder. Into the driving. Into the mauve-colored bridge."

MARINE:
"In our opened heads, the bird of the real!"

AQUAMARINE:
"Love remaining — in a dull, fixed state. Along with the main axes of time. And alternating conditions. Transitions. Into the slime."

MARINE:
"Into the concrete!
It's getting damp. Then, it goes past. Before we've even comprehended it. Surrounded by concrete. Or, rather, a concrete hand."

AQUAMARINE:
"The little lovers remain in a dull, fixed state. After touching the hollyhock.
Then — now, secondhand."

Killing explains nothing — it just shows what it is. It speaks quietly in the presence of blue-clad bone breakers. The singing sounds more precise, and each bit of ecstasy succeeds. Every single one makes an effort. Every single one definitely tries. And it can stay that way, too — if we so choose. A little bird returns in the morning sky behind the cantina. The bird of the concrete. The little lovers remain behind, vacant, and complete. The dog, the pig and

the chicken leave the cantina in boiled order. The blue-clad drinkers and bone breakers obliterate the little lovers' timeless vat and timeless bird-idol with gentle tools:
Hollyhocks, minutes, seconds —
hammers and forceps of an expanded connection, within the concrete and right into the slime, bridge and forceps, objectivity and forceps
and balance —
imbalance in their blows.
These drinkers do their work with lovers' precision.
In doing so, they cry out to the vat: "Who are you?"
And to the little lovers, "Who are the two of you now?" and "Where to now?"
Relieved, they speak, on the sunny side of the cantina.
Illuminated by a yellow flower.
MARINE and AQUAMARINE whisper in final certainty before extinguishing:
"Precision, hollyhocks!"
"Desires, hollyhocks!"
"Details, hollyhocks!"
And shortly thereafter:
"No precision."
"No details."
"And no desire."
Finally, alternately speaking:
"Onto the lead plate, let it be a lead plate that is used for cooking behind the cantina, and smoke the details.

Further blackened gender-details. Within this — this lost-ammonia — understood.

A potassium deficiency. Iron slag.

Why are you so quiet at this very moment, in the atrium, in this controversial atrium?

When it's going past.

Heaven-openings. Heaven-details.

Details, smoking.

Fingers. Toes. Ears.

Evening-fingers. Evening-toes. Evening-ears.

Hollyhock-fingers. Hollyhock-toes. Hollyhock-ears.

Metamorphosis is everything!"

"OF A DESERT DAY"

'Of a desert day'.
And unto it. The blackbird.
Unto elimination.
It is dark (bright). Where it never gets bright (dark).
The glare of the negative.
In telling a story of elimination.
Further back. 'Back'. 'Past'. There are shackles with their lamps. Sago. Something cool. A double-track. 'They lived', 'they didn't know it'.
In endless extension of the desert track of a sand-colored animal, or animal-replacement, in this thundering negative. Glare.
'They didn't know it, that the last'. The negative. 'Ahead'. Sago to the doors of the concave front side and coal-colored walls. Costumes, equations, judgments. Of all facts. 'Past'. In order to try (be silent). In order to change (fail). To destroy everything within that blossoming human-revolution. In order to change and destroy everything there is until it fails. Coal everywhere, from the big travelers, gone, 'all-too-early', with their lamps.

Tweezers.
The blackbird.
And bright cutlery. It's flashing (this worry). Reflecting (this warmth). This warmth of flickering lamps, in a garden. Of permanence. Of human-figures and their replacements in a great, past age. Dandelions. And bright cutlery — white, from discourse. Unto the crime. Of a calf's lung. Along with reassurances. Unto figure-remnants. And gentle crimes. This revolution-cutlery steams forth from the breath of the animals that move between silent feet or 'glance along' and stand still, when you stop, in a delayed garden and in explicit warmth, and I take this revolution-cutlery in my hands and cut through bodies and distant drifts. 'Desert days'. Desert days, unto elimination.
Should it get dark in this brightness (these are final shackles), should it get dark in this explicit garden (it's fatigue), should it be understood (consumed by animals) — what you say until it gets quiet — back-counted — or even it should be silent, well, who will understand or expect understanding? Permanence (sleepers). Until you sit down. In this coal-colored room, there's a proscenium, there are awful wardrobes (Persile), and a lace-floor in the trusted warmth of a hollyhock-filled garden, and it's no beginning (slept), and it's no end (played), and it's no beginning that speaks and no end that closes, it's simply a wave-movement on this darkened human-ocean, and marlins that have gone on ahead are diving there; and

then, soon, it's become the just-past, and soon it's become the smoking present, a groundswell of history that's cutting — human-figures sliced with incisions — 'desert days', into the blue, with their lamps, into a gentleness — when and if I want it to be so.
There are two women next to me, they're sitting on rocky banks with Medusa heads, one on the left, the other on the right, both on the edge of elimination.
Of this view.
Of the blackbird.
Of return-glances. Duplication.
Such a manner of precise glare, of tools, and a manner of true occurrence, they never were and never shall be even if we search for them forever, in a Vermeer — yet they're clotted and lost, there's only minimal permanence (sleep), and there's no beginning and no end, and there's no bright beginning to be set and no dark end, either. 'Past'. Past, of a ambling glance. And of resistance. Of a glance, and its reflection. Penetration and elimination. Electra. Medusa. Carbon. Plankton. MARINE. AQUAMARINE. 'Then, past'. 'Of desert days, later'. Unto the carbon that sits at the ready as it always was and right past a phosphorizing plankton, into the postures of doubting travelers. Marlins. Sago, with their lamps.

It is dark (bright).
In a precise garden.

The flowers speak of resistance against human-revolution. The woman on the left, she crashes, she places her hand on my dry knee as she goes. MARINE. Before me, at a short distance, films play out.
'Bergen-Belsen'. Of the negative. 'Ravensbrück'.
Glare of the negative.
Sago on hands and feet. Further storytelling, and a history that sticks. A sheared-off head promises them improvement, and a sliced-off hand lets them heal. Problems of antiquity, comedy. Shots in sand-colored bodies releasing a nearby-target. Continuing into the smoking present. A story that's being told, that stinks. Mountains of corpses. Certainties. Crematoria. Uncertainties. Blackbird. Little human-figures sent from certainty into uncertainty and opening an intermittent-target. That is, in fact, the final-target. They motion past the intermittent-target with a carbon-hand. And with a plankton-neck. They stink. They illuminate. They reflect. They stink, running quite counter to the completed human-revolution beginning in a hollyhock-filled garden that's uttered quietly in the style of amazed travelers — under burden of proof — under burden of truth ending in a carbon-colored room, with fanfare. Elimination.
Those stories shown at close distance are not visible.
I'm still. A blackbird. Desert days.
For my warm face reflects its blood-past. Risk-time. Revolution-time with hands and feet in a star-covered

manege. With horses, at close distance. They're uttered and stink — for they're burnt, they do not move from their positions, because they're burnt, and everything's burnt, everything's already been burnt and uttered — and disappears. Back. 'Medusa'. Problems of elimination. And, its flammable solution. An intermittent-target that's failed. A final aim. 'Past'. Small human-figures are burnt, with fanfare, and there are dummies. There are blossoming lamps. And they're explicitly so, hollyhock-filled gardens in their warmth seeking out amazed travelers. In order to study this success. Flowers speaking of resistance against final human-revolution. Small human-figures burning right-straight-in near the doors — and back out again by the fireplace. They're being let go. Something cool. They're being duplicated, in that one sees how they're coming and going up in flames, and they're remaining in permanence-clouds above us until they crackle to the ground, ground 'of the desert day' — and we see how they move and disappear into the Sago — yet this story is redoubled for us along with those non-existent true events (in that we're shown how it all comes, and how they're eliminated).

We redouble in viewing this horror — precise flowers that speak of a resistance that cannot succeed — and we're crestfallen when it goes quiet.

It's a breath between animals that move between silent feet or 'graze together', and they snap at my hands. They tug those hands into the bush and their improvement is accomplished beneath the hollyhocks. I sit there with Domitian.

It's a shared breath between blossoming animals — an intermittent goal. A steed's mint. Blooming on the ashes of the burned. The redoubled. And it signals: Who's speaking, and to whom? Who's answering, who's showing these events, and who's going out to meet them? Which one of us is silent in permanence (sleep)?

I'm speaking. Is the steed speaking to the mint, or is it the other way round? Is the breath speaking to the fireplace, or is it the other way round? If what's being said, what's being shown, of the negative, is being understood (consumed). With its lamps — or if this fireplace deviation is too much — and these words issued running off course — yes, farther off course and countered in hollyhock-colored bushes by strangers' hands, and travelers' hands — amazed — in the garden along with explicit human-figures before the image of the Medusa.

More and more we deviate — into a happy fireplace and sago-colored doors — and this story that's being told is being consumed at every turn and those amazed human-figures within them (understood).

And we're off the rails within a mummified hand and breath of elimination.

This worry.

The garden, well, the plans were barely given to me. Soon it's just-past — then the smoking present. Soon I am in Mexico (pre-spoken). A provisional arrangement. Forests. Toucans. Who goes there, however, and waits. Mexican forests (cameras). Pictures. Of the negative. Perforations, close-shots of a bizarre human-revolution. Beneath grazing animals. Blackbird. Of a desert day. The groundswell moving across the ocean. Decorating itself with paper lanterns that I might not deceive them. Before elimination. Fish, after the expiration of the lamps. Misjudged. Misjudged slightly. Into marlins. Some that come, some that go. Double-marlins. Evening Selvas, black manege, of this there is no doubt. The correct animal trainer term: Human-revolution. In meager cities. But, one forgets. Honey-colored pistoleros.

That's new to me. But it works. The improvement. The punishment. The pardon. Judgments, equations.

Always, redoubling.

The Mexican revolution smells like fish, even in sectioned-off carbon-colored rooms, and at a short distance films are playing out, I've fled before it, in as far as I could, but it smells like fish, and I haven't understood a thing (consumed), and I believe they wanted my hands and feet and the breath between the uttered flowers; they wanted to tug at me in the bush near a friendly fireplace, as they say, and well, everything's coming out of the fireplaces now, and every time it runs into the fireplace there's fanfare and final elimination. They would have transformed me into steed-mints. They would have redoubled me. But I fled in as far as I could, fleeing into a cinema, everyone fleeing into a cinema; if liquidation threatens, then there's liquidity, liquidity in the Pacific Ocean, that's where my cinema is, with marlins, and the carbon-colored doors have closed, and at a short distance films are running (Bergen-Belsen, Ravensbrück), but I can't see and I can't hear, and I'm in a precise garden, in its springtime-like warmth, and I'm sitting in an improvement, like always, in a hollyhock-colored bush, along with Domitian, who's sleeping, and I observe the distant, amazed travelers that are crossing the proscenium, carrying suitcases in their hands — with eyeglasses — doubtful, they're carrying stars, and rightfully so, fatigued before this final elimination that's the intermittent goal — and the ultimate goal — that's being trumpeted with fanfare. I'm sitting in the silence, and the doors have closed upon me — and I hear the breathing of animals that have also fled into the cinema — and it is dark (bright), and it is bright (dark) — until you finally sit down and cross your burnt arms in front of your body — until you sit down next to two women, if I so choose — and they always come — if I so wish — and they're sitting on rocky banks with Medusa heads, on my left and right side, their hands on my dry knees, their breath in my face.

Past. Something cool. 'All too early'.

It's bright (dark).
In an explicitly defined garden.
The flowers are discussing resistance against this human-revolution.
The woman on the right, she flashes, placing her hand on my dry knee as she goes. AQUAMARINE. Several snakes. 'She tells her story with snakes.' It gets better. Past. Something about her was not endearing.
'Something about'.
In front of me, at a short distance, films playing.
'Minsk'. Of the negative. 'Katyn'.
The glare of the negative.
Sago to hands and flower-covered feet that continue telling the story further — even as it disappears — and it begins to disappear into a mauve-colored bush, and the children of human-revolution are sitting there. The great class. With their sheared-away heads. And their atomic murmur. Of the negative. There are funerals. Under the leadership of a great, shining friend of the human and executor of the human-revolution. This human-revolution, continuing in the dust of pulverized animals and people, in a precise garden, precise in its nuclear warmth and pliancy, everything bowed before it quieting down, bowing continuing — and even the rambling double-helix and Sago's quiet formula, even it is brought in the

chill, history is brought into the chill, and there's no longer the just-past, nor a blooming present, nor a smoking future, for we're free.
We're saved.
I don't want to deceive you about it.
We're free in liquidating the great class. The earth-eater. We're going past. We're swimming past. We're going over.
We're wearing stars on fur hats that have already waited quite a while to enter this story, and we're carrying stars in Murmansk, Sevastopol, in the Crimea, too. We're carrying stars from wherever it is we came from and to wherever it is we're going. We're sitting in mauve-colored bushes and are amazed. We're doubting. It's getting better. We're telling a story about Electra. We're standing in flames. The bloody end. In a cinema we flee into when it gets too late. At a short distance, films are running (Minsk, Katyn). We hear fanfares of elimination. But it's getting better. Sago on hands and feet and the dust of pulverized animals and flowers, everything is being pulverized — if you wait long enough — before it gets quiet, only the pure sight of a completed picture remaining (asleep), everything being pulverized — if you allow it and remain silent — and, there are improvements, and they'll pulverize us as soon as we leave the coal-colored cinema, and it's late, 'all-too-early', for the punishment, the equations, and judgments of all the facts. We're dreaming of the end

of human-revolutions, and of their tasks. In a bush. We're speaking in a bush, with dolls.
Between our teeth.
Hair of hollyhock-colored dolls between our teeth, a gentle animal passing us by — no horns, no fur — and it doesn't wear the old fur hat from Murmansk with the star, yes, it must be a horse, and before the last one disappears in the final glare of the negative it shall be a horse, and the recollection of a horse, recollection of horse-forgetting, and horse-remembering, and it'll sit before us, its breath in our faces. Then we'll wait until our eyes have closed — and they have to be closed to see the blossoming end that's coming, that's approaching — and if I would like them to, both women are closing our eyes, one from the left, and the other from the right. Blindness as sole protection in a garden, in a cinema, all-too-early.
'Past.
That they would've given me'.
The double-track.

She knows.
About slaughters.
A bright double-track. 'They lived', 'they didn't know it'. And the comment 'they didn't know they're the last ones'. The response is uttered with a brush. A brush against human-dust and distant drifts. The blackbird. The equation of the negative. Of all films that are being shown, of

breathless and blossoming facts. Unto my hat. The exact time. And that I was forgotten to this extent, with a brush, right up to the medium. Between the hat and the exact time.

It is dark (bright). Where it never gets bright (dark).

But this is nothing new. It goes 'past'. A thundering signal in the trace of a desert leading to an endlessness, into a biting nil, into the task. With lizards and their replacements. Commas. Biting human-revolution. Double-nil. But this is no freedom (forgotten). It's a reaction (recollection). I feel weak with this brush. I stink (some alterations). I'm making equations, for peaceful hands. Again, alterations. Pastures. Fur-societies. Fur-wearers with great recollection of a cave, with lamps. The fur hat is nothing more than a memory that I carry with me, the red star, the yellow star, the biting human-revolution that stretches the cool fur hat deep into the story, and it's nothing more than a memory, really. And a thundering crime. A mauve-colored bush. 'Past'.

I hear crimes coming to me for days on end (soft), and I see them getting bigger (disappear) — as second bodies jutting out of me, bodies of a desert day, into the blue.

Duplicated, burned feet and bloody hands with tatters of human-dolls.

As a hollyhock-colored body, in duplication, through threats and crimes.

The second body of final elimination.

MARINE, who's sitting to my left, if I like, in a late-night cinema, animals, sugared, crashing down, from a dome that's open to the skies, honey-colored human-figures crackling on the proscenium, animals bleating — as if they could be seen (soft), as if they could be heard (disappear), but there's nothing to be heard, and there's nothing to be seen, and we're caught in this duplication that's shutting us in, and it's simply a deadlock of moderately formed air and a thundering of circumstances, and how they're surrendering, if you wait, when it gets quiet, if you wait, and again that blossoming duplication, and everything submits to a little meaning and closes again. These human-figures shiver before such strain. They're wearing colorful hoods. They close. They go past one another, these desert days; *she* knows. Of the slaughter.

MARINE grabs my throat with her flower-covered left hand, and her duplicated body twists sideways, her feet in my lap. It becomes quiet. Now, let's see then. The zenith. What's missing? 'The zenith'.

AQUAMARINE grabs my throat with her right hand, her slender feet in my lap. What's missing? 'The feet'.

It gets quiet and it passes. They've thought of this, with pleasure. Double-legged. All parties. At the edge of the woods with its lights. While I'm waiting with my lamps, that I cause to disappear (go past), dreaming 'of the

animals'. A pair of yellow gloves enough for us. 'The free give in'. Precise time. All that's passing, forgotten, hollyhocks at my feet, the political hollyhocks, the blood of the killed coloring them — the political is the duplication, 'political hollyhocks', 'political people', racing in their duplication, blood of the politically murdered falling upon them and they, becoming political, stinking utterly. Fanfare. Everything stinking. Unto elimination. The political, and the duplication. Encounters, and crime. That's easy to say.
Terror and slaughters.
Symmetry without compare.
But as for me, I want to remain untouched (free). I want to remain, without threat, among these women. Women. Left and right. Whenever I want them. With animals extended before me, at a distance, of course — excluding contact —along with hollyhock-colored, precise plants in a midday-garden during a happy, happy time.
I want to be undetermined.
Directionless in particularity.
Beneath mistaken designations. 'Aberrance'. 'Deception'. I want to be deceived (forgotten). I'm deceiving the animals, they extend before me and disappear in a completed picture.
A view.
'Of a desert day'. Unto that. The Blackbird. Unto elimination. Animals devouring me, deceiving, spewing me

out, deceiving and me, disappearing into a completed picture of utter relinquishment.

I stand as an aiding-star in the sky.

We are stars, though (released). We're wearing capes. We're amazed, and bluster about on the proscenium. We move ourselves back and forth, the sky and the paradox Earth of contact, and of crime. A double-track. Sago. Something cool. 'They lived'. 'They didn't know it'.

'Saw it, fleetingly'. 'He stood still'.

In a precise, flower-covered age.

I see hollyhock-colored flowers at my feet while I hold my eyes closed; eyes closed, closed (released) — before me, an elongated dog, a flower-colored zebra, screaming, closing the scene.

We were, however — as our own — our double — we were all as our own — foreign — that should be the basis for a final answer coloring itself black, or a question that colors itself white.

And we're in a cinema, and there, at a short distance, films are being shown, films of all these facts, of all these reflections.

Reflected just until that reflection disappears.

Thundering reflection.

Sizzling disappearance of the lizards. A cutting answer in a precise garden at midday, at the zenith, at the anti-zenith, zenith, anti-zenith of organizations (sleep), of non-organizations (remembrance). I trade the elongated

dog for the screaming zebra. It disappears. I exchange the garden for the cinema. Past. 'Desert days.' Into the blue. We go there now, and scream. We swap small human-figures for their replacements in language — a language of the political, of the negative — but it's only a fiction of the negative, it was only ever a fiction of the political collapsing before our eyes, and the political is not possible, it goes past, and we go past, we disappear before we've ever come, and we wait, 'we go past', 'we wait', remembrance, 'past', we're amazed, we fall, fall into the precise, into a flower-covered age, and we go past with precise animals between our silent feet, they 'graze together', their breaths in our faces.
That closes it, then.
In four pieces.
'Scattered'. 'Free'. 'Going'. 'Cloud'.
Everything else falls by the wayside.
But it's midday.
'It shall'.
'In the sky'.
'Two kinds of animal'.

HAVE MERCY ON US!

December 24th:
"It is well into the crime (I
want to).
An eye on everything.
It's a flower meadow (I would
like to).
I'm in the middle.
Between the end and the beginning. And therefore, duplicated.
Who's going with me?
She was more valuable than all theater (I
can). With steady handles. We cross the ship's deck.
Others absent: 'handles'.
'Ship's decks'.
A tale of the sea.
I was just about to name it (sleep).
I have to collapse everything. And a distant bay.
Crab fishermen. Location lights.
Formby Point. Merseyside.
Have mercy on us!

You want to stop but there aren't any friendly ships
ambles into these difficulties of format, and you want to it
to stop but there aren't any lamps, only 'handles' that no
one uses, human figures strewn about, sea people, cranes,
flower-tonnages,
speech-presentations in precise time.
'You wouldn't know it, that ship'.
Thus, 'that ship'
Has come.
'Or drooping down, Merseyside'.
There it is!
I'm in the middle.
I'm not everything.
I don't reach the bloody beginning nor the smoking end.
'A yellow dog of no use to anyone'.
'Preventing nothing, with
a yellow handshake'.
Who stops me!
If I consider the small space that I'm seeing, and that it's
connected to
the nearest thing ('dog')
and with the most distant ('formats'),
the spirits with precise bodies through an
invisible ribbon of events in a
lemon-colored age.
Who stops me!

December 25th:
"Crimes," answers AQUAMARINE.
"Blossoming occurrences.
Blossoming crimes.
Yes, we're well into these duplicated crimes,
those crimes committed from that bloody beginning,
those 'from the yellow dog' or 'from the friendly ship'
and those that extend right to the smoking end,
'from formats'. 'From spirits'. Equations. Final equations
in a speech-presentation of precise time. You move onto
a friendly ship at a precise time. You move 'across ship's
decks'. With 'handles'. You see Formby Point. You see
Merseyside. See blossoming events that are arriving.
Actually, nothing more than this sort of crime occurs.
In that you're being hit on a head that's blossoming.
These events a skull and crossbones formation on the
deck of a friendly ship that's imperceptible, though precise
in form, yet imperceptible, you see, it's an 'overkill', and
I'm in the middle.
The driving center.
Of a coast covered with gorse.
Formby Point."

December 26th:
"If I like her. We're being warned.
Everything's been prescribed. The external-actions (vehemence). The internal-actions (trauma).

The friendly coaling ship's boarded. At the flower curtain. We're being warned. A second regulation of the garden. We've boarded the coaling ship on the side that seems to be facing the coast. It's illuminated with lamps. Location fires. Sunflowers. The forests on the coast extend to the yellow side of the heavily loaded ship that's sitting askew, and if I'd like, screaming monkeys almost board with people, and screaming people almost go on board with the monkeys (that's it exactly), and the pelican, and the toucans.
(December 16th)
The fog along the coastline, 'the spirits', the unnatural rows of flags, those opened to coastal forests (closets).
Set up, vomit, cook, move two thousand hellish nautical miles away (from death and concentration and revolution), 'hellish' if possible and to the awful crossing of an equation made up of blossoming events yet to be determined. Land-walkers don't return. Move on with lamps.
(December 17th)
Fistfight with sailors. Discussing paradise. A plant-code. The division of sunflowers. The payment. The counter-revolution. The captain is silent.
(December 18th)
Unloaded fifteen yellow shots, used the machete, 'Ship of spirits, spirits linked to precise bodies by events.' What events? Forgotten. Remember. Forgotten (from a flowery drape).

(December 19th)
Surrender the wheel. Lift the sails (emblems). Puke. Cook."
(December 20th)

December 24th:
"Dislocation. Nighttime storm.
Lightning coursing through an opened head. Sunflowers. That's it, exactly.
Seabirds eat. Dictate. Extinguish lamps. Light lamps. Lightning cognacs. The captain, silent. Draw equations deep into the mathematics of stewing external-actions:
'That's all he's written me'.
'Which with open eyes I simply cannot believe'.
'Subordinate everything . . . which I simply cannot believe'.
So that entire sentences might fall away, with their lamps too. So that everything is made possible. Everything! Every lemon-colored situation. And counter-situations as sedations. In all the letters she writes to me (at lower levels), she writes of human-revolution. At higher levels, she writes of flower-nature. To the gorse (shut). To the sunflowers (cries). Her blood-redness flowing right straight through these events. Flower-crimes. At the very lowest levels she says:
"You're within a blossoming human-revolution just as others are happy in their little gardens, you move about

within it, leaning on sunflowers, and you have to collapse everything you encounter (passes you); wherever you are, there final revolution is, too, along with legs and how they move, and greasy hands and how they waver, and animals and how they solace us, right here at Formby Point, Merseyside. Have mercy on us!"
And I say:
"Let it be — that of the space — with its lamps."
Let it be a completed equation of final events.
And I won't go away
and I won't come back,
and I won't go on either.
"When they light up,
they'll jut out (as sunflowers)
(I want to)."
We're all being warned.
What else should I say? I'm in the center. Everything is passing by. I'm not moving out of the center — neither toward the upper end — for that's where the friendly ship is — nor below, no, for that's where human-revolution would be; no, I'm standing right in the center, leaning on a flower and telling this sea story, out loud. In remnants. What else? Until these remnants disappear — like everything's passing — wavering (a flower), or flickering (a lamp). We're being warned, and we're extinguishing our lamps.
It's quiet.

'Extinguish the lamps'.
'Still'.
(I want to)."

December 25th:
AQUAMARINE answers:
"There's an external world (sunflowers).
There's no external world (sunflowers, second class: A friendly coaling ship). Everything's passing by. The stab of a knife. And lupines.
If we connect them to each other, they'll pass us by.
Nothing remaining.
And everything remaining possible.
Have mercy on us!"

REVOLUTION OF THE INTIMATES
(A REPORT)

So, it looked as if this mouth is present in an illuminated age. We were being shot at. We slept down below, near the rudder (mouth). As if this honey-colored mouth that's speaking were hidden in the Selvas, and by looking, you'll find it again, you'll find it again — as if we were traveling downstream in the middle of the flower-covered river. I should've mentioned that. I said,

"Where do I come from, for the opened arm
(stock).
Where do I come from, grasping
that cinnamon-colored hand, hair, ten steps in the wide Selvas, into the groin of that phosphorizing double-woman. The bilingual.
Hearing, and speaking, at the same time.
MARINE. AQUAMARINE.
(Painted stock)."
The double-woman answered:

"Where do they come from for that opened leg, the extra leg at that precise time?
Where do they come from

with phosphorizing hands
(nature-stock)?
You only see an opened eye — not empty hands.
In the underbrush. And those hands move.
On other rocks, as an eye — needing to be shut."
An open height rising from a coastal forest.
A flower-colored scale. In real-time. Then, Maxwell again.
Reason, always:
'Of salespeople. Attendants. Through that'.
Opened scale. Nile-legs. The bilingual. So, I've told myself 'brush', and I've told myself 'go' and said 'if I could clap myself together' and said 'opened'.
I've told myself 'brush that makes the interior within smooth', 'mouth, that opens the interior within', the monkeys calling down from the galleries of the forested coastlines. So:
    "Oven!
It's a ship
(before intimate forests)
It's not a ship before intimates, this revolution of the intimates beginning at the complaint-openings within burnt bodies and moving straight into coils of intimate screams. As an enema. There's no longer a ship (at anchor) before this revolution of the intimates, a penetration into the nearest thing (leg) and into the most distant (scales), uttering a soft washing swishing

in an opened mouth that's muttering —
and closing — that it might rise";
and then — I am sitting on the pavement.
As a first step.
Knowing everything.
Slinging all aside.
Forgetting everything.
Experiencing nothing new.
Doublespeak.
Knowledge, surrounding the opened leg.
Forgetting, and enveloping this opened arm.
The first step into stock.

The others.
It's not here.
'Bells'.
What's happened (ringing).
Everything's missing.
'Republicans'.
Whatever's passing (republican).
Everything writing.
'The plant-colored receipt'. The second step.
We enter the internal with opened bodies (devise). We go into the depths of the Mexican Selvas because of this body-revolution. It begins with an opened scale. With pavement. Tearing me away. Whatever we encounter, we open. Monkeys, children, toucans, women, tapirs.

Everything else fleeing before this. We open the useful. Leaning against the bars (stock). Armed with a machete (the fury has passed). With a compass (methane) and the mass of the presaged.

'Toucans'. 'Boas'. 'Maxwell'. Always a reason-fiction. Human-figures moving. Human-figures riding down open-standing coastal-forested galleries — moving in the smoke of ship's cannons — cannons firing aimlessly at those coastal-forests (the fury has passed). 'Someone hears', 'it all helps', a demand that I listen, a weak demand and assisting, too, and she says 'Tunis', and she goes before me, she says 'about painting', and she crosses the honey-colored river with Nile-legs — old sense forgotten and that final tiredness of these intimates opened in the middle of a fragrant wood, a wood derived of the tiredness of that wood and fossilized love—and yet no love (corned) but a rooftop that's gone past us, an aid, a white bird — everything opened.

That, of past moment. With 'plant-colored receipt'. So: Ten steps to real-time. I *do* have to get old. As long as I know what I am talking about. Everything forgotten. Corned. But I don't know where I'm going ('go'), and I don't know what I'm talking about ('talk'), going and speaking at the same time, hearing and speaking at the same time, and 'a receipt' disappearing from the deck of this ship in the form of a mule.

'Form of a mule', 'the mules', 'the monkeys'.

Not from where. 'I'. The opening.
I'd like to stop, but I'm opened.
A second step.
Corned.
At anchor.
Selvas.
With blossoming thumbs.
In cracks. The smell of blood: 'Then go. Then I'll go into the bog. Then go'. Entering into body cracks — successful — cracks called 'roof' and we go in, in cracks called 'boiled foot' and we enter them.
And we *become* a rooftop and she, she's called 'boiled foot'.
That means.
We become rooftop, although we're in the middle of a human-comedy, and called 'boiled foot'.
There's no escape from this intimacy. Heat. Identicals. We enter into the intimate asleep (the identical) — and we wake up with mule ears on our hands. They're the ears of big steps. Two plant-hours. A green month. All parts. Balsa-hands holding a green piece of paper with a receipt: 'Then go. Then I'm going into the bog. If only I could enclose myself. If only I could exclude myself. Trousers and skirts. Government and revolution. In small depressions. Sheep paths. Goats and goat manure. Then go'.
We wake up with mules on our feet and a bluish machete in the underbrush, taken from a hand (one) or a hat (two)

in mangroves along the shore, or with a charge (three), moving further up along a forested-coast (four) — we chop it all down and let it go up in flames, just as it pleases us, and rolling before us at a constant distance, the cinnamon-colored, bilingual water.

The ship at our back is sinking on the rocks of an unspoken question. And it emerges, having run upon the answer. On board, screaming monkeys. Trousers and skirts. Flags. Government and revolution. In depressions. It hasn't dropped too far. I was hanging on it. It moves mechanically. Kofrosta. Mexican. That means: In circles, everything ending up reversing back onto itself — all coming back past itself in circles and shredded down to its smallest parts, shredded right within these intimates, and we're riding up to galleries on flower-adorned mules — and back down again — and we can choose now, so we wave our arms and call to one another, but we don't see each other, and we don't understand each other, in fact we don't understand anything or anyone, and we understand nothing and no one, and we ride past one another into a clock of the identical, of the intimate, a sliced up and burning clock, and then it seems as if the mouth is locked within illuminated time, and understanding is gone, gone past like a plant-colored question, its answer ensconced in a brightly illuminated age. And we're bleeding for one another and past one another — bleeding in a revolutionary way, and in a counter-revolutionary way, and

we're chopping for one another and on each other, and past each other, and we're circling each other and going right past one another into solitary identical images, and we could choose if we want to rule or to be ruled, if we want to be followers or to be followed, and we see it's all the same, and we stumble in circles, stumble further into these intimates within the powder of the revolution, stumble into other darknesses, into word-revolutions of the intimates — beneath a second, overcast sky — taking a third step.
Corned.
I'm even screaming.
Look!

"What's coming now is intimate-blood!
What happens now means final distillation,"
says AQUAMARINE.
"But then I'll be crashing to the ground, sideways!
Slung into my own arms. An illuminating fire, with a cap.
A children's story.
But then it looks as if that mouth
has emerged in a burning age
(and I think):
New climate. 'The mouth'. The smoldering mouth expanding in the story of these intimates.
I've asked questions, torn up questions as
'fever-person', 'quay silt' or

'silver paper in front of a closed mouth', inhaling everything, 'a fever', 'the mouth'
'the willing-persons!' inhaling everything
and distilling everything, in blood!
The fourth step.
'To intimate-blood!'
It's not an empty promise (gasometer);
It's smoldering,"
says AQUAMARINE.

   "But you have to get away
from the promise. From illuminations. From
quay slime. You have to get away from any picture that
extends itself into this story. Blood-picture. Smolder-
picture.
You have to tell this story, right to the end, with promises.
You have to get away
From the machines and this aquamarine costume
(that is possible).
You have to become ungrounded
(that is urgent).
You say: 'By'.
You say: 'Crane'.
You are ungrounded
(different),"
answers MARINE.
'Fifth!'

Then it appears as if this mouth is present in an illuminated age.

This mouth is ungrounded.

Time is grounded and different.

Illumination hovers. 'The lumberjacks'. I am enclosed.

I am smooth. 'On a summer evening'. That's hovering. I see a honey-colored mouth. Transparent. A long, extended shallowness.

On a frontal corner, with flowers. 'A couch'. We were closed. I need them all!

There were lists, in the black, and in the green of the fog-draped Selvas, and we were moving up the river searching for the intimate. We were sleeping in the rudder compartment (mouth). Horses (opened time), standing on the poop-deck. I said: "We were shot out of the Selvas. In that flower-draped age. The rudder compartment was different. The horses, ungrounded. There was no iron." That was it, exactly. "As long as I was standing next to her, we beat on that crackling rudder compartment. We were moving. The opened ship was too heavy to pitch. It glided." I should have said that. The captain was standing next to me, supported by illuminated flowers. The captain that left the deck. Monkeys with him.

Can you steer?

AQUAMARINE sat on the couch on the fore-deck and said:

"You'll never see him again.

Now, you'll never see him again, never again before disappearing.

The other shoe's dropped. I am enclosed. In an intimacy of words. I am in something. Different. Ungrounded. At the window of the other shoe. Shoe that fell down, into this intimacy. Of the Selvas. Intimacy hidden in the Selvas, saying:

There is no iron.

Just as the mouth that speaks is hidden in the Selvas, so you'll find it there again, you'll see them there again and take them to yourself, and dissolve them. You'll dissolve them. With chalk. In the rudder compartment, with the captain."

We slowly course down the middle of the flower-covered river.

Went there. It's a charge (distillation).

We've been given the task of distilling all we encounter, the monkeys, the river, the Selvas, the rudder compartment, everything! We are enclosed. In our charge. We are careful. We know that someone is trying to distill the others when it's standing still. We are in constant flower-movement. Rudder-movement. A flower-clock. I see the mouth before me (the rudder compartment), how it rises and falls and is driven down the river bend, green hills above me and a long shallowness (of the mouth) on my left, and I see this mouth, and I'm enclosed in something, and it's the intimate. Six steps. Enclosing themselves. Forward

and back. On a summer's evening, forward and backward in the story. Sixth. The charge of distilling. The revolution of the intimates (report). In the opened Selvas. The train conductor. Since she's crying. The loss at sea.
It's completely ungrounded.

"What trains are," answers MARINE.
"Lumberjacks slept.
Otherwise, we have nothing.
We remain different (in occupation).
The truth. The bilingual. Hearing and speaking. The dissolution. We couldn't understand a thing; the distance — enormous. We're the first humans. On a flower-covered river. We are the flower-covered (river).
Principles aren't enough.
They glow.
Distances! Flowers!
They dissolve.
Flower-covered.
I've felt the mouth of the bilingual on me as if he were together, with me, in that honey-colored age.
I'm waiting for the shooting.
Seventh.
It's passing.
I feel the mouth, on my knees."

I wanted to continue. Hair, fog, the mouth,

all on the couch, the boiled monkeys too.
The wood, slowly thinning out, the ship was no longer moving upstream. Circling. 'The hair slipped in' was said. 'The fog waiting here'.
The others displayed a waking (of the mouth). Will they attack? You and the other remain.
In flower-colored time.
We were being shot at.
Then we saw, we heard the mouth encased within an exterior dissonance. And yet we still said:
'Mouth'. 'Hair'. 'Fog'.
Then, everything collapsed, completely.
Dissonance. (8.)

Two man.
'Eat!'
Either. There were no villages (the dissonant mouth).
We turned back. The ship lay askew, in shallow waters.
The captain said: "There is no iron. No wood. That's it, period."
They didn't change a thing. Neither the flower-clock nor that weakly illuminated, honey-colored age.
Just stillness.
Of the mouth.
'Marsh-grass'. The bilingual.
Of whom no one knows any more.
On which dissolution came, from afar.

Dissolved. Nine.

Left, right.
That was her restraint
(of heated mouth)
in disappearing

ABOUT THE AUTHOR

Born in 1963 in Frankfurt am Main, Peter Pessl grew up in Germany and Austria. Since his first book appeared in 1984, he has published a number of volumes of poetry, prose, and radio plays as well as created work for audio spaces, installations, and performances. Pessl lives in Vienna where he continues to write and organize various literary and audio art projects for Austrian radio (ORF).

ABOUT THE TRANSLATOR

Mark Kanak's work and translations have appeared in journals throughout the world. He has published a collection of his poetry in German, *abstürze*, and a translation of Jeff Tweedy's *adult head* (*kopf erwachesen*). He is a recipient of a Gertrude Stein Award for Innovative Poetry from Green Integer Press.

AQUAMARINE
final tales of the revolution

by Peter Pessl

Translated by Mark Kanak from the original German *Blumarine. Letzte Erzählungen zur Revolution* (Klagenfurt: Ritter Verlag, 1998)

Cover and design by Jed Slast
Set in Janson

FIRST EDITION

Published in 2008 by
TWISTED SPOON PRESS
P.O. Box 21 – Preslova 12
150 21 Prague 5, Czech Republic
www.twistedspoon.com

Printed and bound in the Czech Republic by PB Tisk

Distributed to the trade by
SCB DISTRIBUTORS
15608 South New Century Drive
Gardena, CA 90248-2129
USA
toll free: 1-800-729-6423
www.scbdistributors.com

CENTRAL BOOKS
99 Wallis Road
London, E9 5LN
United Kingdom
tel: 0845 458 9911
www.centralbooks.com

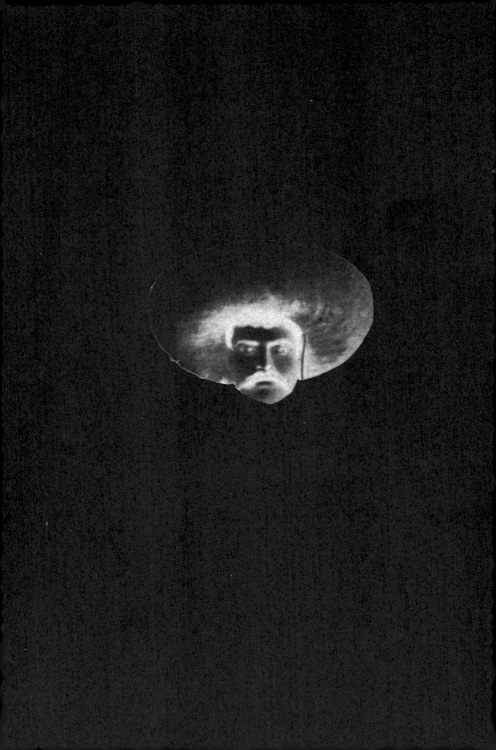